Against All Odds:

A Journey of Hope and Resilience

Mary Fowler Simmons

Contents

Dedication

I want to acknowledge my supportive husband, Barry Simmons, and my children: Makayla, Kiyah, and Mya Simmons. I'd also like to recognize Diane Cotman, Shirley, Hester, Dorothy, Henry, and Joseph. My nieces, Tierra Fowler, Yumika, Shana, Wanda, and Laura, along with my nephews, Brandon, Anthony, Marcus, Terrell, and Andrew, have been by my side during this journey. While I have a large family, I wanted to include all my nieces, nephews, and cousins (Joseph and Elizabeth) whom I did not mention. I'm grateful for the support of my mother-in-law, Alice Simmons, as well as Carl, Brenda, Kaye, Jean, and Enoch.

Thank you, Sharyn M. and Sade J., for your support and for helping me stay focused on my recovery. To Angela D., Tamika, and Kizmet, thank you for loving and supporting me. My visits with Bernita Randolph were always meaningful. She listened to everything I requested and made sure it was done. I know my illness affected her because she lost someone dear to her heart. I was not just her supervisor; I was a supportive friend who became part of her family. We would often discuss world affairs and share our viewpoints on solutions to problems. Together, we made quite the duo in work meetings, laughing about things that didn't make sense in the world. We consistently enforced best practices and professional work ethics.

I would like to thank my church family in Richmond, VA specifically the Deaconate ministry. Patricia Douglas, Frances, Kimberly Lankford, Donna Stallings, Paula Williams (The Diva Deacons). Deacons Si and Brenda Spratley, Justine Jordan, Cynthia Woodson, Deborah Garner, and Donald Chambers. A special thank you to Deacon George Douglas – a great and caring man and my buddy who can't get angry. I would also like to thank Fawcett Publications for their assistance and support in getting the book published.

I would not be alive today without the help of the innovative and fierce leader, Dr. Robert Winn, Director of the VCU Massey Comprehensive Cancer Center. Special recognition goes to the incomparable Keri R. Maher, DO, MS, Director of the Acute Leukemia Program.

Author Introduction

My middle school years were challenging and uncertain. We lost our home in Church Hill due to a fire. My mom searched everywhere for shelter, and lo and behold, we found it with the Housing Authority at Mosby Court Housing. I attended Mosby Middle School and couldn't wait to go to school. I thought moving from a house to an apartment was a challenge.

Our first week in our new living situation was frightening. I had never heard gunfire so close, and I didn't know how to process it. During the day, it wasn't too bad, and I enjoyed playing with the neighborhood kids. I was raised to walk away from troubled people, but that became a challenge as well. I had to learn how to fight to defend myself because you needed a tough exterior to survive in the hood.

I kept to myself during people's conversations and walked away from any potential trouble. One evening, I was playing kickball with my friends, and we sat on our bikes, discussing what to do next. We decided to ride to the convenience store. Suddenly, gunfire erupted, and everyone scattered. We huddled on the side of the building, holding hands, eyes closed, until the chaos subsided.

I just wanted to go home, and I was scared. My friends and I hugged, and we went our separate ways to head home. As soon as we turned the corner, we saw a dead male body on the ground with a gunshot wound to the head. I was only thirteen. I couldn't move for a second; then I jumped on my bike and pedaled as fast as I could to get home.

There was no counseling available for facing and coping with death. I remained in shock because I had never experienced anything like this. I began to notice the drug scene and the so-called glamour associated with that lifestyle. At that moment, I realized that lifestyle wasn't for me. I focused more on my academics and didn't want to go outside to play. I excelled in advanced math, history, and English. When I did go outside, I stayed by the door until the streetlights came on.

Living in public housing affected my self-esteem and exposed me to the social stigma often associated with being a resident. The facilities were overcrowded, sometimes leading to unexpected and negative encounters in our living environment. We faced maintenance issues and safety concerns that impacted everyone's quality of life. As residents, we had fewer economic opportunities nearby, which limited our upward mobility. Crime and a lack of resources were daily struggles, creating a stressful and insecure environment. The willpower and the courage to survive are what we have to do as a culture, turning negativity into a positive. Finally, we received good news—we were moving to a house again.

I will define my life by my journey and the crossroads I have walked. It reflects a strong sense of individuality and determination to shape myself through my choices and experiences, rather than my past or origins. Embracing my journey and the person I become is a crucial part of personal growth and empowerment. My mother, Florence, embodies resilience.

My take on this experience is that it taught me I can weather a storm without fearing anyone or anything. It taught me to be strong in life and to live it to the fullest. This experience showed me that people are not always who they appear to be, so I must remain vigilant. I don't regret this challenge because it taught me to never give up and to turn the impossible into the possible.

The Intro

Psalm 133:1 How good and pleasant it is when God's people live together in unity

Yeah, I'm the baby girl among thirteen resourceful children of Mr. Joseph and Florence Fowler. There are five rambunctious boys and eight demanding, moody girls. My mom is the queen and matriarch of the Fowler family because she didn't take any nonsense from anyone. She was stern and firm in our upbringing. I was spoiled, but I was filled with love and compassion for everyone, especially my siblings. We are all loving, caring, and loyal to our families. We are an African American family that, for a long time, was shielded from the harsh realities of the world's injustices. Our parents kept us in a bubble, and for a while, we didn't see the double standards embedded in the system around us. I watched my parents raise a large family and work hard for every single dime and then some.

My grandmother, Hester, moved in with us after my grandfather passed away, working overtime to make ends meet. She was a strong woman who endured racism but remained steadfast in her focus on the glory of God. Often suffering from swollen ankles, she kept the house in order, cooking dinner and having a special treat for me every night. We both enjoyed chocolate-covered cherries. The holidays were filled with her homemade icing, crust, and sweet potato turnovers. My dad struggled, particularly with alcohol, but my mom held everything together. He endured a lot from childhood to manhood, while she made life seem easy, even when it wasn't. My parents and grandmother faced significant racism at work and had to endure much because they had a family to support. They didn't complain but instead dealt with their disappointments and continued to have faith in God. My mom made our financial hardships look effortless, and we never realized the extent of what they were experiencing. We always had food on the table, a roof over our heads, clean clothes, church, and the Sunday desserts we looked forward to. My grandmother was famous for her sweet potato turnovers with homemade icing and bread pudding.

During thunderstorms, we had to turn off the TV and sit quietly in the living room while, as my mom and grandmother would say, "the Lord does his work." This was often said to calm us down and reduce our fear and anxiety. It conveyed a sense of divine activity during a frightening natural event. This references God's power over nature.

We had each other to play with in the backyard. We had to stay close to the house, but that was fine. We are our own best friends. Neither my mom nor my grandmother liked to repeat themselves when they asked us to do chores or tasks. Bad behavior was not tolerated inside or outside the household. When guests came over, we would talk and then head to our rooms to play games or watch a movie. We were raised under the rule that children were to be seen, not heard, and that was how you showed respect. As the years passed, we lost our grandmother, which left a hole in our hearts, and we had to learn how to keep going without her.

As time passed, my mom had to retire early due to health issues. She became disabled. That's when it was our turn to take care of her and ensure she had everything she needed. We experienced a lot of family loss over the years, which hurt my mom dearly, but she supported us during the difficult times. She would always say, "Never question God because he needs his children back with him and everyone's story must end when God ends it by his grace and mercy." All my siblings are working, my dad has retired, and my parents have each other to lean on for support. They loved family gatherings, especially during the holidays. We had potlucks, long conversations, and laughter. While most people say Christmas is the best holiday, for me, it has always been Juneteenth.

The family would gather to enjoy delicious, down-home Southern food, playing football (girls vs. boys), volleyball, kickball, and cards while listening to soulful music. We were rich in heart because we had each other. My mom's favorite holiday was Mother's Day, as she was showered with gifts, steak, seafood, and anything else her heart desired. She was overjoyed when my brothers gifted her a full-length black fur coat to complement her small stature. Did I mention my mom was only 4'10" and weighed 120 lbs.? The girls gave her clothes and shoes, while my dad presented her with jewelry. My mom is filled with compassion and love; she is supportive and very vocal, always expressing her thoughts without hesitation. Our queen is spoiled with love because she deserves it. She is our backbone, the reason we remain connected. When faced with tough decisions, we always turned to her. She always knew just what to say. She'd listen and then tell us, "I know you left something out, but here's what I would do." Oh, how I miss my mom's words of wisdom and would do anything to keep her nearby. God was the source of our life and love.

Josephine, the eldest of thirteen children, adored her only son, Ricardo, and would give him the world without a second thought. Joseph, the oldest son, has children who serve as his support system, helping him navigate life's challenges. Juanita had one devoted son, while Charles was blessed with three beautiful and clever daughters. Laverne had three sharp-witted young ladies and a fierce son. Bernard had no children but treated his nieces and nephews as if they were his own, celebrating them on every occasion. Fonz, my brother, was murdered in Richmond at the age of nineteen, and it remains an unsolved case. This murder deeply affected our mom's spirit, yet she remained strong. Hester had three diligent young men, and Shirley had a self-reliant son. Dorothy had two passionate young men, and Diane Cotman had a supportive, dazzling daughter named Tierra Fowler.

As for me, I have three ambitious young ladies: Kayla, Kiyah, and Mya Simmons. We've had to mourn a lot. We lost Josephine, Juanita, Laverne, Charles, Bernard, and Fonz. We also lost two nephews who deeply affected our family. Each loss changed us. But we held onto one another so we could stand tall.

My childhood was amazing and adventurous, as our financial struggles were kept from us. My mom skated with me, played hopscotch, rode a bike, played marbles, and Jack Rocks. She would consistently beat me and my neighborhood friends in Jack Rocks because she was the master of all my childhood games. I couldn't envision my life without her, as my friends knew I had a cool mom since she made time for me, even when she was exhausted from work.

The challenges of my childhood revolved around learning to appreciate what I had. My older sisters passed down their gently used clothes, and my parents contributed to my wardrobe whenever they could. My sisters were responsible for cooking dinner, while my brother took care of maintaining the yard and taking out the trash. There were no options or substitutions for food. If you didn't eat what was on your plate, you simply wouldn't eat at all. My parents worked hard, and wasting food wasn't an option with thirteen kids.

At twenty, I felt as if my life was beginning, until I received the emergency call that my mom wasn't responsive. It left my heart bleeding and aching. I had to ask God to pull me out of the darkness because I knew my mom would want me to keep going and not remain stuck in time. I did not understand this terminology at the time, but I came to grasp it as I matured.

Mom, you are missed

Although it seems like yesterday

The pain has not been dismissed

Mom, you are missed

The memories, your scent and your touch are what hold me together

There is no other like you

Your laugh and advice linger in my head what would you do

Mom, you are missed

This grief and pain are with me today and forever more on earth

Time is moving and I just want you to know your worth

Mom, you are missed

After that, the losses continued to accumulate. We were still grieving when death struck us again, and we had to support each other through wave after wave of sorrow. My dad's heart was breaking, and honestly, we didn't even realize how deeply it affected us because we were too immersed in our own pain. It felt like our minds and bodies were not functioning, and how does one recover from losing the nucleus of the family?

Ten months later, our father passed away as well. I remember the times when my dad was sober; he would take me downtown to shop and show me where he worked. We would explore different parts of the city together, walking hand in hand. He would say he needed to protect me in this cruel world, keeping a firm grip on my hand. Afterward, we would have lunch, my ice cream treat, and catch the bus back home. I truly cherished our father-daughter days, as they were precious moments. Even in death, our mother's voice remained with us. She always made sure we were supportive, encouraging, respectful, and loving toward one another. She raised us to stand together, no matter what life threw our way. A family that prays together stays together, and we continue to live in unity.

***

As a young adult, I adored children and was passionate about them. So, when I became pregnant and delivered a stillborn baby boy, it shattered me. I was told I could not have children, and my heart broke into a million pieces. This experience had painful emotional and psychological effects on me as a parent. I had to acknowledge and allow my grief, seek support, and remember to honor my child. My physical and emotional well-being was crucial, especially during times of intense grief. I became involved in activities that brought me comfort and helped me set healthy boundaries.

As time passed, I became pregnant again with a baby girl, but she did not survive either. I sought a second opinion, and I was advised to undergo a surgical procedure called tubal ligation, as it was not suitable for me. Carrying a child was considered unwise due to pre-eclampsia, but I prayed. I cried. I asked God, *Where is my grace? Where is my chance?*

And then I got pregnant again, and this time, I made it through with Makayla. I had no medical issues. It was a blessing beyond words. My whole family rejoiced when I had her because they knew what it meant to me. My mom was not living and would want family to step up in her place. Diane and Juanita were with me in the delivery room. They were both stubborn and excited, as my husband had no say in this matter. My husband couldn't take the sight of the birthing as he kept upchucking and was dizzy. It was Juanita's birthday, and that was her birthday present—witnessing her niece's birth. Diane refused to work and came straight to my side to see this miraculous blessing. Look at this picture; God said otherwise, and I gave birth.

Then came Kiyah, followed by Mya—a total of three young ladies.

I'm satisfied and grateful for my blessings. I know I was meant for something bigger, and I've always been a competitive person.

During my adulthood, my sisters bonded and formed strong alliances in our sisterhood. We continued our weekend gatherings, just as our mother wished. Most of the time, Diane, Shirley, and I would play cards, dance in the house, and reminisce about our childhood. Occasionally, Hester, LaVerne, and Dorothy joined in the festivities. In front of the apartments, we organized kickball games that captured the interest of our neighbors, who joined us. Then we started a football team, and the neighbors were intrigued, as our family was a jack-of-all-trades. Simple fun was a part of us, and it shone through.

Finding work became a challenge, as I was unaware of how things were when I thought the slavery mentality had ended. I faced prejudice and discrimination in the workplace. I was passionate about my job and performed it well. I worked twice as hard to demonstrate my dedication and work ethic. I participated in every training session and gained a thorough understanding of the company's policies and procedures. I wrote the department's standard operating procedures to ensure my division was compliant and could pass audits for grant reconciliations. I continued to invest my energy in my job, and I was hurt when I was overlooked for a potential promotion because I didn't fit the management image. I had the necessary education and years of experience. The person who got the position needed help with the work, and I was chosen to assist, or rather, to be a team player. I could have handled the entire job and delivered results, but I wasn't considered good enough for the position. This was an unfair situation with no pay increase. I had an outstanding performance and produced a high volume of work with no errors. I communicated with management, but it led nowhere. I continued to provide for my family and held my head high. I trusted my manager, despite the lying to staff about procedures and my work ethic. The years of trust became unbearable, and the relationship became irreparable. This was very stressful; I had to take medication for my blood pressure, and my diabetes medication increased. The challenges before me affected my health, and the system remains broken.

I was a great family member, friend, and mentor. I was an active listener to understand goals and challenges. I showed empathy by understanding how to connect on a personal level, recognizing and validating others' struggles. My relevant experience has provided a solid foundation of knowledge, enabling me to offer valuable advice. I have approachability and accessibility, making it easy for others to seek support. I encourage independent thinking to promote ownership of their learning and development by motivating others to explore new ideas and solutions. Honesty and integrity are important to me because I must look at myself in the mirror. I strive to maintain transparency, building trust and respect in all my relationships. Maintaining a positive attitude and enthusiasm inspires me to help others. I always communicate with patience, respect, and constructive feedback, which are essential qualities of a supportive individual.

One night, my sister Diane had a spiritual visit from my grandmother, who told her I was sick and might pass away. Diane was upset and restless, so she called me to tell me to get help if I was ill. I thought I was just dealing with pneumonia and found it very concerning.

Chapter 1
The Challenge

Romans 5:3-5 Not only so, but we also glory in our sufferings, because we know that suffering produces perseverance; perseverance, character, and character because God's love has been poured into our hearts through the Holy Spirit who has been given to us.

For weeks, I kept telling myself it was only a stubborn sinus infection. Spring pollen always teased my allergies, so I bought the usual over-the-counter drops, brewed honey-lemon tea, and promised my body I would slow down "tomorrow." Tomorrow never came. I still rose before sunrise, packed lunches for the girls, and answered emails from the kitchen counter while the kettle whistled. Even when the coughing fits woke me at night, I rolled over, whispered a quick prayer—*Lord, settle these lungs*—and tried to drift back to sleep.

The infection dug in deeper. By the second week, I could feel a heaviness in my chest, as if someone had stacked books on top of my lungs. My voice grew raspy. As I read morning Scripture at the table—Psalm 91, my refuge psalm—the words scraped out thin and breathless. Makayla noticed first.

"Mom, that cough sounds different," she said, brows knit in worry.

"I'm fine, baby. Just need more rest," I answered, waving her off with a smile I didn't quite feel. Mothers do that. We reassure while our own knees shake.

Barry watched me climb the stairs one evening, one hand gripping the rail, the other pressed against my chest. By the time I reached the landing, my pulse hammered so loudly I could hear it in my ears.

"That's it," he said, voice gentle but firm. "You need to get checked."

"I will, after laundry," I joked, even though the sight of the laundry basket made my head spin.

Each day, the small tasks took larger bites out of my energy. I tried telehealth first, hopeful that a stronger antibiotic would chase the infection away. The nurse on the screen listened, prescribed, and reminded me to rest. I nodded but kept moving—washing dishes, answering calls from my Sista Diva Deacons, jotting grocery lists for Barry to pick up after work. Productivity felt like proof I was still winning.

Then came the morning my right eye clouded over, vision splintered at the edges like cracked glass. I blinked hard, but black patches floated across the room. Fear slid up my spine. I sat on the edge of the bed, lungs tight, whispering,

"Lord, is this pneumonia? Is it something worse?"

The house was quiet; the girls had already left for school. I pressed both palms over my heart and tried to slow the rhythm, tried to find the calm in Psalm 23: *He restoreth my soul… He restoreth my soul…*

When Barry walked in from work, he found me still sitting there, folded over like a wilted flower. No more jokes, no more bravado. I looked at him and said, "I can't catch my breath." That was all it took. Within minutes, he had the keys in his hand and a bag ready for the emergency room that included phone chargers, insurance cards, and a small bottle of anointing oil my sister Pat had given me last Christmas.

As he guided me to the car, the porch steps felt like a mountain. Each breath rattled. I wanted to cry, but held the tears for later. I whispered over and over, "Jehovah Rapha, my healer… Jehovah Rapha, my healer." Every exhale felt like a plea and a declaration all at once.

The drive to the hospital blurred past storefronts and traffic lights, and I could barely focus on anything. Barry reached across the console, squeezed my hand, and said, "We're almost there, baby." I tried to nod, but my head felt too heavy to lift. All I could do was breathe…and pray…and believe that God was already in the ER waiting for us.

That was the road that led me to the hospital doors in April 2022.

What began as a sinus infection had turned into severe pneumonia. I could barely get out of bed; even making it to the bedroom felt like a struggle. My chest felt very heavy, and I tried to stay calm because I thought I was having a heart attack or a stroke. My eye was glossy, and it looked like it had been shredded. When I blinked, I saw black patches in my vision. We waited patiently for the hospital to run tests, which included blood work and a CT scan. The wait felt endless. It was a long time before the doctor returned with any results. I couldn't eat or sleep, as my weak body ached, which made me restless.

The doctor eventually returned to inform me that I needed to get a CT scan with and without contrast. He also mentioned that I would soon be assigned a room. I went ahead and completed the testing to get answers. I told my husband to head home and rest, and that we could discuss the results in the morning when the doctors made their rounds at 7:00 a.m. But then everything changed; my future was in question.

The team of nurses and doctors rushed into my triage room, asking me questions, clearly confused about how I was able to function and why I was not unconscious. The chaplain came in to pray with me. That's when I received the kind of news that shatters the ground beneath me.

The big "C" word.

Cancer.

The Grand Reaper.

When most people hear the word "cancer," the first thought is, *I'm going to die*. This crippling disease had spread throughout my body, putting me in a delicate space between life and death. The doctors estimated I had one to two weeks to live. I was told to get my affairs in order.

I don't remember the next few minutes. I think I nodded. I think I thanked the doctor. But it all moved in slow motion. I was hearing people speak, but their words felt like underwater noise. I sat there, breathing shallow, trying to make sense of my own body. My hands had started shaking. My throat felt tight, like I was swallowing cement.

The machines kept beeping softly beside me. Normal sounds, but they felt louder than ever. I could hear the squeak of nurses' shoes outside in the hallway. I could hear the rustle of someone pulling a curtain. I stared at the IV tube running from my arm and wondered how something so thin was supposed to hold me together when everything inside me had come apart.

I didn't cry right away. I sat in silence. And for a moment, I felt numb. Like I wasn't even in my own body. Like I was watching someone else get the news.

But then the thoughts came fast. *Do I tell my daughters now? What if this really is the end? Did I hug them long enough last week? Did I tell them everything they need to know?*

I reached for my phone, then stopped. Who do you even call when your world has cracked open like this? How do you find the words?

I turned instead toward the window. It was late afternoon, the light dipping gold against the glass. I remember thinking how strange it was that the sun still shone so calmly. That outside, people were walking, traffic lights were blinking, families were probably ordering takeout and watching TV. And yet, here I was, sitting in a bed with a countdown placed on my life.

I whispered, almost without thinking, "Lord, I'm scared." That's all I had in that moment. No rehearsed prayer. No polished scripture. Just the truth.

That quiet whisper was my first real prayer that day. I didn't ask for healing. I didn't ask for a miracle. I just needed God to hear me, right where I was. To find me in that small space between fear and surrender.

That first night alone after hearing the news felt unreal. I was in shock. Completely lost. It was like I was stuck in someone else's nightmare, except it was happening to me. I kept blinking, hoping I'd wake up and realize it was just a bad dream, but I didn't. I couldn't stop replaying the words in my head: "one to two weeks." Over and over. Like they were branded into my mind. I'd never felt that kind of stillness before. That kind of silence that makes your skin crawl because your world just split in half. How do you even process something like that? I kept thinking, *How is this possible? How did I even get here? What did I miss?* It was like the air had been knocked out of me, and no matter how hard I tried, I couldn't catch my breath. My body was in the bed, but my spirit was somewhere else entirely. I stared at the ceiling for what felt like hours, and nothing around me made sense anymore. I didn't know if I was supposed to scream or stay quiet. I just lay there, frozen.

Everything was quiet, but my mind was screaming. I didn't know what to do. I didn't know how to tell my girls. I didn't even know how to tell myself. I felt like I was watching my life play out from outside of it, like I was hovering over the room, trying to hold the pieces of myself together while everything was falling apart. All I could feel was the weight of fear pressing down on me… heavy, cold, and sharp. I laid there with tears in my eyes and no words left in my mouth. Nothing I had ever gone through in my life prepared me for this moment. Not the hood, not heartbreak, not loss. This was different. This felt like the edge.

And then, somewhere in that silence, somewhere between panic and heartbreak, I heard myself start to whisper Psalm 23. "The Lord is my shepherd, I shall not want..." I don't know where it came from, but it rolled off my tongue like muscle memory. "He maketh me to lie down in green pastures... He restoreth my soul." I whispered it over and over again. That Scripture became my oxygen. My steady rhythm. The only thing anchoring me. It was like I was floating, and the Word was the only thing keeping me from slipping away completely.

I asked God for grace. Not answers. Just grace. I didn't even know what to pray for. I wasn't asking for healing. I wasn't asking for a miracle. I just needed Him to be close. I needed Him to sit with me in that room and hold me up because I didn't have it in me to stand. Because in that moment, it was just me and God. No doctors. No husband. No children. No distractions. Just me and the One who still had control, even when I felt like I had none.

I told Him I was scared. I told Him I wasn't ready. I told Him that I didn't want to die. I told Him that I wasn't done being a mother. That I still wanted to see my girls grow up, walk across stages, build lives, and become women. I told Him I still had dreams. That I still had things to do. I told Him I felt robbed. I told Him I was angry. But I also told Him I was listening. I told Him that if this was going to be my walk, then I needed Him to walk it with me. Step by step. Hour by hour.

That night changed something in me. It broke me down to the rawest part of myself. But it also opened me up to hear Him in a way I hadn't before.

I called my husband and told him what the doctors had said, but I wanted us to tell the girls together in the morning. I asked the nurse to call my sisters, Shirley and Pat, to deliver this heartbreaking news. Then, I sent a group message to the rest of the family. That was one of the hardest things I've ever had to write.

I was just devastated and numb inside. I couldn't even cry, and the room was spinning. Before they moved me into my room, my niece Tierra showed up. I saw her before she even said a word. Tierra walked in quietly, but everything about her said she wasn't going anywhere. Her overnight bag was slung over her shoulder, her lips pressed together, and her eyes… already full. She was holding it all in, but barely. That's the thing about Tierra—she wears her heart right there on her face, and she's never been good at hiding it.

She didn't say "Hi." She didn't ask questions. She just pulled the chair close to my bed and sat down. Her hands were shaking, just like mine had been earlier. She didn't reach for me. She just sat there, as if she made one wrong move, she'd fall apart completely. I tried to turn toward her, but my body was so tired, I could barely shift. I opened my mouth to say something, but no words came. What do you even say to the person who loves you like a second mother when you've just been given a death sentence?

I looked at her, and I saw my own fear reflected back at me. That broke me more than anything. Not the diagnosis. Not the pain. But seeing how much this was hurting her. Tierra is strong, bold, and fierce. She's the kind of woman who walks into a room and people notice. But that night, she was a little girl again. My little girl. And I couldn't do a thing to protect her.

She wiped at her face, fast and rough, trying to act like she wasn't crying, but I saw it. Her shoulders trembled. Her foot tapped the floor like she needed somewhere to run, but didn't want to leave me. And I wanted so badly to grab her hand, to tell her that I was going to be okay, even if I didn't believe it myself. But my arms felt like cement, and my body just wouldn't cooperate.

"I'm fine, baby," I finally managed to whisper. But we both knew it wasn't true.

She turned her head away so I wouldn't see her tears, but I saw them anyway. The way they slid down her face without a sound. And that silence said more than words ever could. She was grieving me before I had even left. And that realization nearly split me in two.

I've been in Tierra's life since the day she was born. From diapers to dance recitals, I've seen her grow, fall, rise, and shine. She's never known a world without me in it. And for the first time, I realized she might have to. That's the kind of pain that doesn't announce itself. It just settles in your bones and waits.

The nurse came in, soft-spoken and careful. She glanced at Tierra and then at me and said, "She needs to rest now." Tierra stood up, nodded, and kissed me gently on the forehead.

As she walked out, I closed my eyes and silently prayed, "God, hold her for me. Wrap her up in strength where mine has run out."

I had to get ready for the battle ahead. I needed to prepare my family for what we were about to face. And I had already made up my mind. I was not backing down. Giving up was not an option.

***

There's something about a group of praying women that makes the earth shift. That's what the Sista Diva Deacons were for me. A force of faith, of love, of no-nonsense encouragement. We didn't just gather for prayer, we gathered for war. Spiritual war. And they showed up like an army, ready to tear down anything that dared mess with one of their own.

That afternoon when they came to see me, I was curled up in that hospital bed, feeling like a shell. Weak in body, drained in spirit. But the moment they walked through that door, I felt something lift in the room. Like oxygen. Like sunlight. They came in with food, Scripture, and jokes. I'm telling you, we didn't even need a preacher; we had our own pulpit right there beside my IV stand.

Pat, my rock. Kim, the quiet storm. Paula, the one who will call out heaven and hell in the same breath. Donna, the backbone. Together, they didn't just pray, they shook heaven until it listened. Donna took my hand, and before I knew it, they had formed a full circle around my bed. No one said anything for a minute. They just stood there. Hands joined. Eyes closed. And the room got still.

Then Paula started humming. Low at first. It was "Break Every Chain," and before long, the others joined in. My spirit stirred.

Something in me woke up. And when they started praying, it wasn't soft or sweet. It was fire. Scripture flew through the air like arrows. Donna was swaying. And me? I just laid there, crying. Not out of fear. But out of release.

They prayed over my body, my blood, my bones. They prayed over my daughters, my husband, my doctors. They called healing by name. They asked the Holy Spirit to flood every hallway of that hospital and sweep through the building like wind. And I believed them. Because I had to. Because they did. Because there was no room for doubt in that room.

That visit didn't just lift me, it changed something in me. It reminded me that I wasn't alone, and I didn't have to carry this cross by myself. That no matter what came, I had sisters who would fight beside me, cry with me, and feed me soup when I couldn't lift a spoon.

Later, when they left, I felt stronger. Not because my pain disappeared, but because I remembered who I was and who I belonged to. I wasn't just a patient. I was a child of God. **1 Corinthians 13:4-5. Love is patient, love is kind. It does not envy, it does not boast, it is not proud. It does not dishonor others, it is not self-seeking, it is not easily angered, it keeps no record of wrongs.**

However, that was short-lived. My mind was still spinning long after they left. The scent of oil was still on my skin, the echo of prayer still circling the room like a breeze that wouldn't settle but inside me, something heavy refused to move. I laid there looking at the ceiling, and the question kept pressing in. "Why me?" I wasn't trying to question God's authority. But I was human, and I had to ask.

I thought about all the good I had done in my life. I thought about every Sunday morning I made it to church, even when I was tired, even when I had to drag my girls out the door and make sure their hair was done, clothes ironed, and breakfast cooked. I thought about the times I tithed with money I needed for bills. The times I stood in a food pantry line, not for me, but to serve. The way I always tried to check in on somebody else, even when no one checked on me.

I thought about how many prayers I'd whispered on behalf of others. How often I poured out love and compassion even when I didn't have much to give. I was a daughter, a wife, a mother, a worker, a servant. I gave my heart to people and my soul to God. And now, this?

I said to God, "I'm not perfect, Lord, but I'm Yours. I show up for You. I work for You. I try my best to walk right, love people, forgive fast. So why this road for me?"

And still, the silence came. Not an absence but the kind of silence where you know He's listening. Just letting me speak. Letting me cry and shout and whisper all in the same breath.

I thought about the pain, yes. But I also thought about my daughters. My beautiful girls, who were still growing, still learning who they were. Who would guide them if I left? Who would be their safe space if I weren't here to hold them up? Who would understand their silence, their sarcasm, their dreams? The thought broke me.

I felt robbed. Like something had been taken from me without warning, without fairness, without mercy. I wasn't asking to be immune from struggle, I just wanted to know why this one. Why this storm? Why this cross?

I clutched the sheets as if they could answer me. But all I heard was the quiet rhythm of the machines and the slow drip of the IV.

As I sat alone in that hospital room, it felt like life had thrown a dozen curveballs at me all at once. I felt rage building inside me. I had to knock some things down, scream, and tell my God what was on my mind. So, I asked Him, *"Can I speak freely? Because what I'm feeling may not come out gently."*

What did I do to deserve this? Why me, God? Do I have a future or not? What about my children?

I want to see my kids graduate. I have goals. I still have things to do. The tears finally came, and I began pounding the pillows to release the fiery rage inside me. I grabbed the nearest pillow and slammed it into the bed, over and over, until my arms were shaking. I yelled, not words, not sentences, just the kind of sound that's been buried too long. The kind that doesn't come out pretty. I had kept it together for everyone else, but I couldn't anymore.

I screamed into the pillow. I pounded my fists into the mattress. I shouted up at the ceiling, not in defiance, but in desperation.

"God, do You hear me? Do You see what this is doing to me?"

I was angry that I had to be the one sitting in this bed, watching my life slip through cracks I couldn't even patch. I was angry that I didn't feel strong, that I didn't feel chosen, that I didn't feel ready.

"Why this storm? Why now? I'm tired. I'm tired, God."

There was no one else in the room. Just me and the raw sound of my own heartbreak. And maybe that's what I needed. To stop pretending like I had the kind of strength that didn't cry. To let myself be small for a moment. To be the daughter in need of her Father.

I collapsed back into the bed, breathless, my arms limp, the pillow still clutched in one hand. My chest burned from the shouting, but oddly, I felt lighter. Like something had been peeled off of me.

Then, something lifted, as if a burden had been taken off my shoulders. My tantrum was over, and I was exhausted. I'm a fighter. I'm a doer. *Tell me what you want me to do, and I'll do it.* That moment forced me to put my faith to the test. I had yelled, I had cried, and now I had to walk through the storm with my eyes open. I straightened my back, wiped my tears, and whispered to myself, "You've been through too much to stop here." My head wasn't held high because I felt strong—it was because I was choosing to believe I could be.

That night, I felt something shift in my spirit. The room was still, but inside me, things were being rearranged. God didn't answer me in thunder. He didn't speak in a booming voice. But He made His presence known in the stillness. And in that silence, I started to reflect on my life—not just the good parts, but all the places where I had poured myself out for others, forgetting to pour back into myself.

I saw how I tried to be everything for everybody. I had spent years listening, fixing, showing up, carrying, and never once thinking that maybe that wasn't always my job. That maybe, just maybe, I had been stepping into roles God never assigned me. I had confused being helpful with being responsible. I thought I was being obedient, but I was inserting myself into spaces where only God could move.

I thought back to all the late-night phone calls, the last-minute runs to help someone else, the emotional weight I carried on behalf of people I loved, and people who weren't even pouring back into me. I called it service, but truth be told, I had neglected myself. I didn't make room for rest. I didn't make room for reflection. And I surely didn't make room for healing.

God showed me that clearly.

It was like a movie playing behind my closed eyes. Moments where I chose others over myself. Times I said "yes" when I was already empty. I thought it was love, but I realized that part of loving others is knowing when to let God be God. When to step back and trust that He doesn't need me to be the fixer—He just needs me to be faithful.

And I had to own that. I had to face the truth that while I was trying to be strong for everyone else, I had been weakening my own spirit.

So, I let go.

I said, "God, I surrender it. All of it. The people, the weight, the expectations. I can't carry it anymore. I was never meant to."

That surrender wasn't dramatic. It wasn't loud. It was quiet and slow, like exhaling after holding your breath for too long. I didn't feel instantly better. But I felt honest. And that was the beginning.

He showed me where I had intervened in His work, trying to help people when He was the one meant to fix things.

I thought I was helping. I really did. I thought I was following God's plan by stepping in every time someone needed me. I believed that being available, being dependable, being "the strong one" was my assignment. But I had to learn that sometimes, helping isn't the same as healing. Sometimes, the best thing you can do is step back and let people go through what they need to go through—with God, not with you.

People must weather their own storms, just like I was learning to do. I used to think I was doing God a favor by carrying the burdens of everyone around me. But He showed me clearly—I was interfering. I was trying to fix things that weren't mine to fix. I was inserting myself into the role of healer when God never asked me to. All He ever asked me to do was trust Him and be faithful in my own lane.

I began to see all the ways I had been drained from an empty cup. Times when I skipped my own doctor's appointments because someone else needed a ride. Times when I didn't sleep because I was too worried about other people's problems. When I gave money I didn't have. When I said yes out of guilt, not love. I wasn't being a servant; I was being drained.

And in all of that giving, I forgot how to love myself.

Not in a selfish way, but in the way God commands us to. "Love your neighbor as yourself," He said, but I skipped the part about loving me. I didn't speak kindly to myself. I didn't nurture my body or my spirit. I didn't ask for help. I just kept moving until I broke.

And it wasn't until I was sitting in that hospital bed, drained of my energy and strength, staring my own mortality in the face, that I realized just how far I had gone without ever refilling myself.

I had been surviving, not living.

So, I asked God, "What now? What do I do with this?" And His answer was clear.

Refill.

Refill your cup with Me. With prayer. With quiet. With truth. With nourishment. With rest. With the kind of love that doesn't cost you your soul. The kind of love that heals.

I had to stop prioritizing everyone else and finally start prioritizing myself.

Not out of bitterness. Not out of pride. But out of obedience. Because if I didn't start choosing myself, I would lose myself. And I knew God wasn't done with me yet.

So I asked Him, not for a miracle or even for strength, but for a fresh start. A chance to live better than before. To choose differently. To move with purpose. To walk in balance. To let Him lead, instead of me dragging myself through the fire and calling it faith.

I had a self-pity party, but then I had to ask, "Now what?" I couldn't live in that space forever. That wasn't who I was. I had already been through too much, seen too much, survived too much to give up now.

So I got up, mentally first. Then spiritually. My body wasn't ready to move yet, but my heart was. That was the first win.

I started talking to myself out loud like I was coaching my own soul.

"You're still here. You're still breathing. So there's still purpose on your life."

"You've got daughters watching you. You've got people praying for you. Don't fold."

"God brought you through every other storm. Why wouldn't He bring you through this one too?"

I reminded myself of everything I had already overcome. From childhood challenges to losses that could've broken me, to all the moments where I was the one holding everyone else up. That woman wasn't gone. She was just buried under pain, and I was ready to dig her out.

I told myself, "You may be in a hospital bed, but you're not buried. This is not the end. This is the reset."

That was the moment I chose to fight. Not just for my health, but for my wholeness. For my future. For my calling.

I needed to get up, stand up, and fight because it was going to get ugly before it got pretty. That's just how life is sometimes. But I wasn't alone. I had a whole army behind me. My God had already assigned angels, family, friends, and even strangers to lift me when I couldn't lift myself.

He had given me the strength to rise like the phoenix that I am... ash-covered but fire-forged.

I could hear Him saying, "I'm not finished with you yet."

That voice echoed inside me, stronger than the fear, louder than the doubt. And I believed it.

"I've still got footprints to put down," I whispered back.

So I made a decision. I would adopt the mindset of a soldier on God's battlefield. I would armor up with Scripture, discipline, prayer, and grace. I wouldn't waste my energy trying to appear strong; instead, I would focus on becoming strong from the inside out.

If I had to cry, I'd cry. If I had to crawl, I'd crawl. But I was going forward. I had to. Too many people were depending on me, not just to survive, but to show what survival really looks like.

I wasn't going down without a fight. And this fight—this one—was personal.

God had surrounded me with warriors. My family, church family, my sisters in Christ, my prayer circle. They didn't just encourage me—they covered me. There's something powerful about being seen as more than a patient. Being treated like a whole person. Being loved like a daughter of the Most High.

And my medical team didn't just run labs and check vitals. They listened. They gave me space to be honest, to feel, to ask. I thank God for the nurses and doctors who reminded me that healing isn't just physical, it's emotional. It's spiritual. It's daily.

Through every high and low, through every pain and every praise, God kept showing up. I started to see that love wasn't just in grand gestures. It was in the prayers whispered behind closed doors. In the meals dropped off on doorsteps. In the quiet moments when I was too tired to speak, someone sat with me anyway.

God's love has been poured into our hearts through the Holy Spirit, who has been given to us.

And I was holding onto that promise with both hands.

Chapter 2
The Walk

Psalm 16:11 You show me the path of life in your presence there is fullness of joy; in your right hand are pleasures forevermore.

My stay at Henrico Doctors' Hospital marked the beginning of what I now call a walking miracle. An X-ray was done on my back, revealing a large mass. I remember the way the technician kept glancing back at the monitor, then at me, then at the screen again. The room was dim, and the table beneath me felt cold against my back. I could hear the hum of the machine and the low chatter of nurses in the hallway. But what caught my attention most was the pause. The long, uneasy silence after the image loaded. She didn't say anything right away, but her face said it all. Something wasn't right.

I turned my head slowly and asked, "Is everything okay?" She gave me that polite smile professionals give when they don't want to alarm you. "The doctor will speak with you shortly," she said gently. My heart sank.

When I got the news that they found a large mass, I didn't even know how to react. I was already drained from the pneumonia, still aching and exhausted, and now this? A mass? I didn't know what kind. I didn't know what it meant. But the word "mass" sounded heavy, like it had weight. Like it had power. I sat on the edge of that hospital bed, praying under my breath. I asked God to be with me, even though my mind was spinning.

They decided to transfer me to VCU Medical Center for more tests and cancer treatment. My husband held my hand as I was being wheeled out, but neither of us said much. The silence between us wasn't from a lack of love; it was from fear. I remember thinking, *God, I don't know what's next, but I know You're already there.*

Once I arrived at VCU, they performed the same scan again, this time with and without contrast. I lay there with my eyes closed the entire time, whispering, "God, show Yourself." That was my prayer. Just those three words. *God, show Yourself.*

And when they came back with the results, I could barely believe what they were saying. The mass they saw before? Gone. No sign of it. Like it had never been there. The doctors were puzzled, genuinely confused, and I sat there in awe, knowing exactly what had happened. That was nobody but God. That was His signature. His way of showing me that I wasn't alone in this fight.

Right then and there, I decided to start walking in that kind of faith. If God could make a mass disappear, He could carry me through this diagnosis. I didn't know what was coming next, but I knew who was walking with me through it.

What are clinical trials? They are research studies involving people that aim to test the safety, effectiveness, and possible side effects of new medical treatments, drugs, or therapies. These trials are crucial for developing new medical interventions and are carried out in different phases. Clinical trials help researchers and doctors understand how therapies work and determine safe and effective doses. This leads to new and improved treatments for patients. Being knowledgeable about the disease can significantly improve outcomes for an individual's life. If a patient chooses to participate in a clinical trial, informed consent is required. This allows individuals to decide whether a clinical trial is suitable for them.

Saying yes to a clinical trial isn't as easy as just signing a form. It's not just paperwork. It's a decision that pulls at every part of you, your logic, your fears, your history.

As a Black woman, I didn't walk into that decision blindly. I walked into it carrying the weight of what's been done to us in the name of science. I knew the stories. I knew how people who looked like me had been used, poked, observed, mistreated, and then erased from the credits. That history doesn't leave your mind when they bring out a clipboard and ask you to sign something that could affect your life.

I sat in that chair with the pen in my hand, pausing. Not because I didn't want to live, but because I understood this decision had layers. I asked questions, then asked more, and finally asked again.

I wasn't going to be rushed or made to feel like just another patient in the system. I needed to know everything: what was happening in my body, what the risks were, who was behind the research, and how it might affect me long-term.

More than anything, I needed to feel that my life mattered to the people giving me care. I needed to trust that I wasn't just a case number or a data point in somebody's report. That's why I kept praying on it. I told God, "If this is the road I'm supposed to walk, I need You to light the way."

Eventually, I felt peace settle in my spirit. I didn't feel rushed anymore. I felt reassured. This wasn't just about me saying yes to medicine. This was about me saying yes to hope, yes to more time, yes to walking in the purpose that God still had for me. And when I signed that paper, I didn't sign it out of fear. I signed it with faith.

Consenting to a clinical trial is your right, your voice, and your choice. The bridge of trust was broken in the history of African Americans because we were not treated equally. For example, in 1951, a young mother of five named Henrietta Lacks visited The Johns Hopkins Hospital complaining of vaginal bleeding. Upon examination, Jones discovered a large, malignant tumor on her cervix. Although Mrs. Lacks ultimately passed away on October 4, 1951, at the age of 31, her cells continue to impact the world. Although these were the first cells that could be easily shared and multiplied in a lab setting, neither the discovery nor the distribution of HeLa cells was sold for profit, and she does not own the rights to the HeLa cell line. The accountability is disappointing.

In New York City, African American and Latino foster children were enrolled in experimental HIV/AIDS drug trials by public hospitals and pharmaceutical companies. Consent was often vague or bypassed altogether. Some of the drugs were still being tested, and children experienced serious side effects, including death. Whistleblowers and journalists later exposed the experiments from the 1990s to the 2000s.

Therefore, there is a wide range of health abuses connected to African American history, where individuals have been used as guinea pigs and experimented on without consent. I extend my support to those who have suffered injustice.

Clinical trials are currently innovative and constantly evolving with new technologies and approaches that enhance the research process, patient care, and the development of new treatments. My recent clinical trial lasted three years, and now my data has contributed to a new, improved trial that takes only one year to complete.

Equality for all people is a fundamental principle that emphasizes the importance of treating everyone with fairness, respect, and justice, regardless of their background, identity, or beliefs. It advocates for equal rights and opportunities in various aspects of life, such as education, employment, and participation in society. Promoting equality involves addressing systemic injustices, challenging discrimination, and ensuring access to the resources people need to thrive. This principle is crucial for building inclusive communities and fostering social cohesion.

Now it was time to stand up and kick cancer in the caboose. I will begin my clinical trial, asking God to walk with me, and I shall not fear. I tried two clinical trials, but they didn't work, and I was given the option to go to Philadelphia for treatment. My preference was to stay in Richmond, VA, to have family support. The physician from Philadelphia consulted with me on my treatment plan. I started the clinical trial immediately; it was scary, and I still had concerns about the side effects.

That's when I met Dr. Keri Maher—one of the biggest blessings on this journey. The first time I laid eyes on her, I didn't know what to expect. I was guarded. Not because of her personally, but because I had been poked, prodded, and processed so much already that I didn't think anyone else could surprise me.

But Dr. Maher was different. She came into the room calm and collected, but not cold. She didn't rush to speak or take over the conversation. Instead, she sat at eye level, looked me directly in the face, and said, "Let's take this one step at a time." That's when I knew—this wasn't just another doctor. This was someone who respected what I was carrying.

I asked her one thing right from the beginning: "Please be honest with me. Don't sugarcoat it. If I'm going to walk through fire, I want to know how hot the flames are." And without hesitation, she nodded and said, "I can do that." From that moment forward, I felt something settle in my spirit. I knew I was in good hands, not just medically, but spiritually too.

She explained my diagnosis—Acute Lymphoblastic Leukemia—with the kind of clarity that didn't make me panic. It made me prepare. She broke it down step by step, and I listened, not just with my ears, but with my whole heart. I needed to know exactly what I was up against.

And I needed to trust the person walking me through it.

I specifically asked Dr. Maher to perform all my biopsies because I could feel her genuine care in how she handled even the smallest procedures. She didn't treat me like just a number or a checklist. She was thorough about hygiene, explained everything as she went, and always made sure I understood what was happening. When you're in that vulnerable position, you cling to those who make you feel seen. And I saw God working through her.

Even during the hardest moments, when I was tired, frustrated, or just plain scared, she would look me in the eye and remind me, "We're in this together." She didn't talk at me; she talked to me. She always asked, "How are you feeling?" not just "How are you doing?" And those little things? They matter. They make the difference between feeling like a statistic and feeling like a soul.

To this day, I believe God placed her in my life at the exact moment I needed her. She's not just my doctor, she's a vessel of grace, a calm in the chaos, and a partner in this fight. With her on my side, I didn't just feel hopeful, I felt empowered.

***

The clinical trial treatment was called HyperCAVD. I received 24-hour chemotherapy for several consecutive days. The first four months were mostly a blur. I was caught in the whirlwind of hospital routines—IVs, infusions, transfusions, beeping monitors, whispers in hallways, the sound of nurses walking fast but trying not to seem urgent. Everything started to blur together; days into nights, prayers into pain. But somewhere in the middle of all of it, my soul stepped out of the hospital room and took a walk.

I don't know if I was dreaming, somewhere between awake and asleep, or if it was a vision from God Himself. All I know is, one night, I found myself on a beach.

The sky was dim, soft, like dusk was folding in. The ocean stretched wide and endless, but it didn't scare me. There were no crashing waves, only a steady rhythm that matched my breath. I looked down and saw the sand beneath my feet, warm and soft, even though I couldn't remember arriving there.

I started walking. Not rushing, not searching, just walking. Each step felt like a release. As if with every footfall, I was letting go of something heavy: fear, anger, confusion, grief. The silence wasn't empty. It was full. Full of presence, full of meaning. I couldn't see God, but I could feel Him. Like He was right beside me, step for step, not saying a word but speaking louder than anything I had ever heard.

I kept walking.

I didn't know where I was going. I just knew I had to keep moving forward.

That's when the glimpses began. They weren't full scenes, not exactly. More like impressions—quick flashes of my life. My girls laughing at the dinner table. My husband driving to work in silence. My niece praying beside my bed. The quiet strength of my sisters. These memories weren't loud. They didn't demand attention. But they reminded me why I had to keep going.

I saw the parts of me I had ignored, the parts I hadn't healed. My flaws. My regrets. The things I buried under busyness or brushed off with, "I'm fine." God showed me all of it—not to shame me, but to free me. To tell me that I didn't have to carry it anymore.

I stopped walking.

The ocean breeze wrapped around me like a blanket, and I fell to my knees. I said, "I'm sorry, Lord. For not resting. For not listening. For not believing that I was enough. For thinking I had to fix it all myself." And then came the peace. A wave of it. I felt it enter my chest like breath.

I heard no thunder, no voice from the clouds. Just the gentlest whisper in my spirit: You are not done yet.

Then, I felt hands—not visible ones, but undeniably real—cup the sides of my face, and I felt life breathe into me. I woke up crying.

But it wasn't a cry of pain this time. It was a cry of being restored.

***

I was awake and felt nauseated, often vomiting without warning. My body didn't feel like my own anymore. Some days, I couldn't even keep water down. Every smell felt like a threat. A tray of food would come in, and my stomach would turn before it reached my bedside. My taste buds changed so much that even my favorite meals no longer brought comfort. That loss—of taste and small joys—was its own kind of grief.

But in the middle of that fog, I remember Pat.

My sister in Christ.

She came into my hospital room like peace in human form. I was curled under a blanket, weak, fighting off sleep and nausea. She didn't talk too much. She didn't try to cheer me up with fake smiles or pretend things were okay. She just opened her Bible and began to read aloud. Her voice was steady, warm, familiar, like home. I don't remember what passage she chose that first time. Maybe Psalms. Maybe something Paul wrote. All I know is, it reached into me and gave me something I didn't know I needed. It wasn't just scripture; it was a lifeline. I closed my eyes while she read and let the words wrap around my pain like a bandage. When I drifted off to sleep, I could still hear her voice in the back of my mind, whispering truth over my weary body.

Then there was Makayla, my baby girl, holding my hand like she was the one trying to keep *me* strong. I was supposed to be her protector, her guide, but in that room, she became mine. Her hand never let go, and I could feel the weight of her prayers in every touch. She didn't cry in front of me, at least not then. She just whispered, "You're going to get through this, Mama. I know you are." And when I couldn't talk, I just squeezed her hand back to say, "I hear you. I'm trying."

During the day, I FaceTimed Kiyah and Mya because visitation was limited. That was one of the hardest things, being separated from my babies. Not being able to touch them or hug them. I had to watch their faces through a screen, trying to sound stronger than I felt, so I wouldn't scare them. They'd tell me about school, about little things happening at home, and I'd nod, trying to smile through the pain. But just seeing their faces, even virtually, reminded me of what I was fighting for. They gave me breath.

I remember my sister Diane asking what I needed and bringing it. Always. She brought me pancakes, my favorite. It was like she had reached into my childhood and pulled out something that reminded me of who I was before the illness. She didn't just drop it off and go. She stayed. She sat with me during her lunch break, and even came back after work when she could. Just her presence was a balm. She didn't have to say much. Her being there *was* the message: "I'm here. I see you. You matter."

And then there was Marcus, my nephew. His visits were quiet, and maybe that's what made them so calming. He didn't ask too many questions. He didn't try to fix anything. He just sat beside me and let me feel like a person again, not a patient, just me. Even when I was anxious and tired of the endless procedures, just having him near settled me a little.

I was upset that my husband couldn't visit as often as I wanted, but I understood. He had responsibilities, work, and the household. He was doing all he could, and I knew that. The day he brought me soup from Panera Bread, I cried quietly when he left. Not because of the food, but because I knew he had driven out of his way, past exhaustion, just to make me feel thought of. He always had a way of pulling me out of the negative and redirecting my mind toward peace. Even when his heart was breaking, he masked it with gentle stories from home—what the girls were doing, how the house was holding up, little silly things. He tried to bring a piece of the world I missed into that room, and I needed that more than he knew.

Brandon, my nephew, came to visit as well. He said we talked, but I don't remember many of those conversations. Chemo fog does that—it steals memories. But just knowing he showed up? That meant a lot. It said, "You're not forgotten."

My sister Dorothy came because she needed to see me with her own eyes. She didn't want updates filtered through others. She needed to witness how I was doing, whether to believe it or not. And when she looked at me, I saw the worry written across her face. But I also saw love.

Each visit was a thread in the net that kept me together. Some I remember clearly, others are a blur. But they all mattered. They reminded me I was still alive. I was still loved.

My husband looked at me with heartbreak in his eyes, though he tried so hard not to show it. He would sit beside my bed and talk about what was happening at home—what the girls were doing, how the laundry was piling up, and how the house still didn't feel the same without me in it. He wanted me to believe everything was okay, but I could see it—the way his voice cracked sometimes and the way he looked away when my eyes started to close. That pain was heavy in his silence. Still, he showed up, carrying the weight of our world on his shoulders while trying to be my peace inside that hospital room.

And I thank God for him.

He didn't always have the words, but he gave me presence. He didn't always know what to say, but he gave me comfort. And that's love—not grand gestures or fancy phrases—but being there when it's hard, showing up even when your own heart is breaking.

Deacon Donald Chambers made sure my spirit stayed nourished. He didn't come empty-handed—he came with the Word, with prayer, with time. I don't think he knew how much it meant to me that he kept showing up. Even when his own plate was full, he found time to pour into me. That kind of dedication? That's ministry. That's the love of Christ in action. When you're sick, you remember the ones who stand in the gap for you. He was one of them.

My mentor, Deacon Barbara Palmer, lifted me in prayer daily. She didn't need reminders or updates. She knew when to pray. She carried me spiritually when I didn't have the strength to carry myself. I could feel her prayers in the quiet moments, like wind moving through the cracks of a tightly shut door. Soft, but undeniable.

Bernita, always dependable, made sure the family was holding up. She became the glue. She checked in, offered comfort, and made sure that even when I was away in the hospital, the rhythm of life at home didn't fall apart. I was so grateful for her steadiness.

Lisa showed up every Sunday with hot meals and dessert for my family. That kind of consistency—especially during a time when everything felt uncertain—was like someone placing bricks under our feet so we wouldn't sink. Every plate of food was more than just nourishment. It was love delivered in Tupperware.

My sissy, Sade, didn't just offer love—she offered provision. Financially, mentally, emotionally. She gave from the heart and made sure I didn't have to carry the weight of my birthday alone. That catered dinner she provided didn't just fill our bellies—it made me feel *seen*. Even when everything about me had changed, she reminded me that I still deserved to feel special.

Deacon Cynthia Woodson was juggling her own responsibilities, caring for her parents, but she *still* found time to feed both my family and my spirit. She didn't just drop off a meal—she brought peace with her. She reminded me what it meant to give even when you're stretched thin.

And my sisterhood—the Diva Deacons. My ride-or-dies. They didn't just pray with me or bring meals. They brought joy. They brought laughter into rooms where tears had been sitting too long. They created bonding moments when I needed something to remind me who I was beyond the illness. When we came together, it was like holy fire—fierce, warm, unstoppable.

Deacons Jordan, Si, and Brenda Spratley brought love in quiet ways. Support in unspoken moments. They didn't need to announce their presence. They just *were*. Their consistency was a gift, their kindness a balm.

Deacon Crawley, when she shaved the last of my hair, didn't just do it as a task—she made it a moment. A sacred one. She looked at me with so much grace and told me I was still beautiful. I believed her. I don't know if I would have without her.

Kizmet, oh Kizmet, with her fuzzy socks and cozy blanket and little gifts. She made me feel human again. Made me feel *whole*. She didn't let me drown in hospital gowns and fluorescent lights. She brought earrings, brought treats, brought light. And she claimed me loud and proud—"That's my sister." You couldn't tell her otherwise.

Avis came with quiet grace. Her visit wasn't long, but it was heartfelt. And my friend Vanessa—her calls reminded me that there was still life outside those hospital walls. That there was still joy, still friendship, still *me* waiting on the other side of this fight.

Each one of these people helped stitch me together when I felt like I was falling apart.

My inpatient stay was challenging, but over time, that hospital room started to feel like a second home. Not because I wanted it to be, but because I had no choice. The walls that once felt cold and unfamiliar slowly began to hold memories. The hum of the IV machines became a background rhythm to my days. Nurses came and went, vitals were checked every few hours, and the fluorescent lights overhead never quite turned off. There were times I'd wake up confused, wondering what time it was, what day it was, and why my body still ached so much.

That morning was one of the hardest.

I had received platelets, magnesium, and a blood transfusion during the night. My sleep was broken, scattered between nurses adjusting my medications and my body trying to rest through it all. When the sun finally started to peek through the edge of the window, I already felt off. Not just tired, but drained. Completely empty. Like my body was trying to keep up with a fight it hadn't trained for.

Then the nausea hit me. It came without warning, without mercy. Just a slow wave at first—and then the crashing kind. My stomach turned at the smell of breakfast. The tray hadn't even been lifted, and I already knew I couldn't stomach a single bite. I asked my nurse, Riley, to move it far from me. She set it over the sink with such care, like she already knew what was coming.

Before she could even finish checking my vitals, it happened.

I didn't even have the strength to reach for the barf bag. My whole body seized up, and I threw up all over the floor. I think I might have gotten some on her shoes. My legs felt like jelly, and I knew if I had tried to move, I would've collapsed. The force of it had me seeing stars, and I remember praying, *Please God, don't let me faint.*

I was mortified. Embarrassed. Weak.

I hated feeling like that—so out of control, so far from the woman I knew myself to be. But Riley didn't flinch. She didn't rush out of the room or show even a flicker of frustration. Instead, she moved with such calm, such kindness. She knelt down to clean it all up, and I could barely meet her eyes. I was choking on apologies, but she just looked at me and said, "It's okay. You can't help that you're sick. It will be alright. Just sit still while I clean this up, and I'll get you cleaned up like new."

I felt terrible about the mess I had created, but I had no control over it.

The VCU Massey Comprehensive Cancer Center made my stay comfortable and calming, providing a safe environment for me.

What a mighty God I serve, and I am thankful for His blessings. This reconnects me with my favorite gospel song, "Worth" by Anthony Brown:

You thought I was worth saving

So, you came and changed my life

You thought I was worth keeping

So, you cleaned me up inside

You thought I was to die for

So, you sacrifice your life

So, I could be free

So, I could be whole

So, I can tell everyone I know

Every day posed a challenge to beat the odds. I underwent a bone marrow biopsy, a lumbar puncture with methotrexate chemotherapy infused into my spine, and I received a bag of chemotherapy while walking twenty-five laps around the unit floor on the same day. Out of everything I had to go through, the bone marrow biopsy tested my faith like no other. I knew it was necessary to figure out my treatment options, but nothing could have prepared me for what that day felt like. Just hearing the word "biopsy" was enough to make my whole body tense. When they explained the process, I felt frozen inside. I remember lying on that table trying to be still while Dr. Maher worked, and all I could think was, Lord, please don't let this break me. I was wide awake during most of it, and I could feel the pressure, the digging, the discomfort deep in my bones. I tried to be strong, but I'd be lying if I said I wasn't scared. My spirit was shaking.

I closed my eyes and started praying. That's all I had in that moment, just me and my God. I asked Him to help me hold on, to steady my breathing, to carry me through. I kept whispering, *This is just a step.* Even though my body was weak, I couldn't let fear win. I needed to know what we were dealing with. I needed to know how to fight. And sometimes, that means letting them dig deep, literally, so you can rise higher.

But it wasn't over. After the biopsy, I had to have a lumbar puncture to make sure the cancer hadn't spread to my brain. That procedure, too, shook me. The thought alone, that something could reach my brain, was terrifying. They had to inject chemotherapy directly into my spine. I tried not to think about how close they were to my nervous system. I remember holding my breath, clenching my fists, and praying not to move an inch. And while Dr. Maher was impressive, that day took everything out of me. I felt vulnerable. I felt exposed. And I felt tired of having to be strong all the time.

I was so close to breaking. I honestly didn't know if I could make it through. My body was in pain, my spirit was tired, and everything in me wanted to shut down. But even in that lowest place, something inside me held on. I gave Him my pain. I gave Him my fear. I told Him, "Lord, I can't carry this. You're going to have to take it." And He did. Not all at once, but just enough to keep me going. Just enough to remind me that I wasn't alone.

With my doctor's approval, I got an exercise bike in my room. That little piece of equipment became more than just a way to move. It became a symbol of hope. I would get on it daily, even when my legs trembled or my body begged me to stay in bed. I wasn't trying to prove anything to anyone else. I was fighting for me. For my health. For my future.

After my bike sessions, I'd walk twenty-five laps around the unit floor. The hallway made a full loop like a circle, and I'd take each turn slowly, sometimes steadying myself on the railing, sometimes walking with my IV pole like it was my race partner. Nurses and patients would wave, and I'd nod or flash a tired smile. It didn't matter how I looked. I just needed to keep going.

On those walks, I saw so many patients lying still in their rooms, curtains drawn, eyes full of pain and exhaustion. And I understood that. I lived that. But something inside me said, don't just walk for yourself. Walk for them too.

So I did.

Some days, I would stop and speak to them. I'd say, "Come take a walk with me. Even just two laps. Let's try." And sometimes they would. Slowly. Shaky. But they moved. And afterward, I'd see it. The little glimmer. The shift. Hope returning to their faces.

I wasn't a doctor or a nurse, but I knew how to love people through the pain. That was my ministry in those hallways. I'd speak life into whoever needed it. I reminded them, this shall pass. You are not forgotten. You are not alone.

It helped me too. Encouraging others gave me strength I didn't even know I had. It helped me set goals for myself and lifted my own spirit. Because when you're fighting for your life, sometimes you need to be reminded that you're still living. That your voice matters. That your faith can carry not just yourself, but others too.

But I also had to learn to protect my peace.

There were moments when the weight of the world felt too heavy. When negativity tried to seep into my room like smoke under a door. And I had to be intentional about keeping my space clean. Not just physically, but spiritually and emotionally.

I avoided gossip. I turned off conversations that didn't uplift. I read my Bible every day. I did devotionals, wrote in my prayer journal, and played worship music softly in the background. I wrote down the names of people I was praying for and focused my mind on healing.

I refused to let bitterness take root. I had already seen what negativity could do to the spirit, and I wouldn't let it make a home in mine. So, I created rituals of peace. Candles. Scripture. Stillness. I prayed over my room every night before sleep and thanked God for bringing me through another day.

Discussing the highs and lows each day, even just with God, helped me stay grounded. I poured it out to Him. My fears. My weariness. My gratitude. All of it.

My main goal wasn't just to heal my body. It was to build my soul stronger than it had ever been. To improve myself from the inside out. My body was weak, but my spirit was in training. And every lap, every prayer, every moment of grace was preparing me to walk forward into a new life with God leading the way.

Chapter 3

The test and challenges

Philippians 4:6-7 Do not be anxious about anything, but in every situation, by prayer and petition, with thanksgiving, present your requests to God. And the peace of God, which transcends all understanding, will guard your hearts and your minds in Christ Jesus.

During my stay at the hospital, which oddly felt like a mini vacation, I was finally forced to rest. I couldn't take care of myself the way I usually do. I needed that rest, that deep care, even though I didn't want to be there.

I missed my bed and just wanted to be home with my family. However, I had to push myself to think about mind over matter.

One day, as I turned over in bed, I noticed my hair on the pillow. I cried because this journey suddenly felt very real. And before I knew it, I had lost most of my hair within a week. It was fast, and it hit hard. I remember looking in the mirror and just... staring. The person looking back at me didn't feel like me. My face looked sunken. My eyes were tired. I looked weak. That's what scared me the most. How fragile I looked. Not just sick, but like a part of me had disappeared. I tried to smile at myself in the mirror, but I couldn't hold it. I turned away.

I always took pride in how I carried myself. My appearance was a reflection of how I faced the world—strong, well-kept, put together, even when everything around me was falling apart. And now, here I was, looking like a stranger to myself. My eyebrows, my lashes, my hair—gone. No warning. No choice. Just gone.

It wasn't just about beauty. It was about identity. It was about strength. I didn't recognize the woman in the mirror, and for a moment, I wondered if she had anything left to fight with. I wrapped my head in scarves. I tried wigs. I rotated between hats and turbans. But deep down, I missed my reflection. I missed feeling like me.

There were moments when I felt so defeated. I would lay in that hospital bed and just cry. Not because of the physical pain, but because of how invisible I felt. I didn't feel seen. I didn't feel beautiful. I didn't even feel like a whole woman. And that tested my faith in a way I hadn't expected. Not because I doubted God's love, but because I had to find a new way to love myself.

Slowly, day by day, I started finding pieces of myself again, not in the mirror, but in my resilience. I had to remind myself that I'm more than what people see. I'm more than the hair that used to flow or the lashes that used to frame my eyes. I am still me. A warrior. A mother. A woman walking through the storm and still standing. And I had to trust that God saw me even when I couldn't see myself.

I learned more about my clinical trial plan, which was divided into phases, with the odd numbers corresponding to the even numbers. Even numbers became manageable, but the odd numbers presented a challenge for me. I kept a journal of how each phase affected me and my body throughout the process. I was able to communicate my status report with my doctor.

Once a month, I was allowed to spend a week at home with my husband and children. That time was precious. I got to sleep in my own bed and soak in a hot tub. It felt strange, but it was the best sleep I had had in months. As soon as I became accustomed to the peace of that little taste of everyday life, it was time to return to the hospital. My children grew sad and withdrawn because of this schedule in my healing journey. I felt sorry too. But I also knew my energy was low. I could feel it in my body. I recognized it was time for my treatment since I had run out of gas like a car.

Each month, I continued to educate myself about my treatments, learned all my medications, understood how each one was administered, how to flush my PICC line, and how often I needed each dose. I always ask what I am receiving before it is administered to me to confirm accuracy. You must be proactive in educating yourself about your health. You must find your voice and use it.

I had to deal with depression because I had been working since I was 14 years old. This was the longest I had ever been out of work, except for when I had my children. I felt helpless, as if I had no voice—Invisible. Useless. I wanted to work, but didn't have the energy. Even paying bills online exhausted me. But maybe God was trying to tell me something. Perhaps that's why He sat me down. I thought about my family finances and reflected on how my God has been carrying me this far, and He will continue to be by my side. I released my burdens to my God, but I wanted them back because they weren't taken care of immediately. I don't like this heavy burden. I asked God to forgive me. I gave the burden back to the Lord and surrendered all. I don't know how I got through things, but my God did it all for me. My God provides for all my needs as I love Him.

***

Chemo brain was another challenge I had to face. I struggled to remember the names of people, songs, and tasks. One evening, I had a video chat with my niece, Tierra, and I could recall parts of the conversation, but I found it difficult to stay on topic. I couldn't even express myself clearly, as the words wouldn't come out as I intended. I went to my sister's house to play cards and be active. A family member asked to change a five-dollar bill, and I replied that I might have it. The family member chuckled, which made me feel foolish in front of everyone in the room because I had to relearn how to count money, and my comprehension had suffered due to chemotherapy. I kept my feelings to myself, but I didn't want to be around people after that. Then someone else, an associate of the family, remarked that my face looked fat, which was due to the steroids I was taking. I didn't receive an apology, but it's true that people can be insensitive. I would chastise myself for not remembering, and I had to face the battle alone once more. I needed to educate myself about cognitive therapy because I'm a soldier, and I'm ready for the challenge to win.

I would play memory games, read, and watch Wheel of Fortune and Jeopardy, as I had to relearn these skills from scratch. I had the willpower to be proactive, but I knew it would take time to build myself up. My takeaway from this situation is to respect people because you don't know their story behind the scenes. If you can't lift up a fellow sister or brother with confidence, don't speak at all. The old me might have clapped back. I would have said something sharp and mean in my earlier days, but I won't go back. I've come too far. I chose a better path to avoid negativity and maintain a peaceful environment. I choose my space of joy, and I find happiness every day. I do not depend on anyone to make things happen for me; I am a go-getter, and I choose to put my faith in God. Each day, I work on building my confidence and engage in my own mental and physical therapy. This battle is between me and God, and I stay focused on the mission He gave me.

Living each day and being able to accomplish even the smallest tasks felt like a blessing. I started cooking again, doing light household chores, and paying bills; that felt like more than enough. I also bonded with my children by simply listening to how their days went and what they were dealing with. My husband isn't much of a talker, but he began to open up about his days, his feelings regarding life dynamics, and the challenges at work. We worked through it together, and he told me he felt better. I thank you, God, for keeping my husband strong because he could have run away from this crisis we faced, but he stood by his family. Initially, he was shaken, isolated, and withdrawn. He took on health insurance and finances to keep our family moving. Makayla stepped into the big sister role like a pro. She helped run the household while maintaining an A average in college. Kiyah and Mya kept their honor roll status in high school and college throughout this challenging time. My children had each other, and they had a family behind them.

God, You have shown me the path to life, and in Your presence, my life is filled with joy. **Psalm 139:14 I praise you because I am fearfully and wonderfully made; your works are wonderful, I know that full well**

Chapter 4

I'm still standing

2 Chronicle 20:17 You will not have to fight this battle. Take up your position; stand firm and see the deliverance the Lord will give you, Judah and Jerusalem. Do not be afraid; do not be discouraged. Go out to face them tomorrow and the Lord will be with you.

It is never up to man to decide whether you live or die. That decision belongs to God alone, because He is the One who knows the whole story from the first page to the last. I kept that truth close to my heart while I walked through the second year of my clinical trial. The protocol would last three years altogether, and even though my body was growing a little stronger, strict isolation was still my reality. COVID, shingles, norovirus, measles, seasonal flu—any germ carried the threat of setting me back or ending my progress. So I lived in careful separation from most of the world and trusted God to keep writing my story.

***

Sunday mornings used to mean getting dressed in my best outfit, meeting my church family at St. Paul's, hugging necks, and adding my voice to the choir of believers. Now worship took place on the small screen of a laptop balanced on a rolling tray. At first I worried the distance would thin the presence of God, but He showed me that geography never limits Him. I would log on ten minutes early, settle my Bible next to a fresh notebook, and wait while the countdown slid across the video stream. The opening hymn played through tinny laptop speakers, yet still filled the room.

Pastor Lance would greet the online congregation and read the focus Scripture for the day. Many Sundays, the passage felt chosen just for me. A verse about healing. A reminder that God is near to the brokenhearted. A promise that the same power that raised Christ lives in us. While the choir sang, I wrote the Scripture in my notebook, reading it aloud under my breath until the words felt stitched into my spirit.

Bible study happened on Wednesday evenings. I printed the outline ahead of time and highlighted every phrase that spoke to my life at that exact moment. Sometimes I shared the notes with the nurses who paused at my doorway, curious about the packets of paper covered in bright ink. More than once, a patient down the hall asked if I had an extra copy, and I was happy to slide one under the door. Even separated by isolation rules, the Word made us feel like family.

There was one Wednesday lesson on Philippians, the chapter about peace that passes understanding. Pastor asked us to think of a time when God's peace showed up in a situation that made no earthly sense. I closed my eyes and saw the hospital ceiling where I first whispered Psalm 23. Tears warmed my cheeks. Right there in an online meeting room full of silent participant squares, I lifted my hand and said, "I am living that verse right now." The chat box flooded with prayer hands and hearts. I felt God wrap me in a blanket of community, though no one else sat beside me.

***

Most mornings started at seven. The overhead lights clicked on, and the nursing team stepped in with thermometers and blood-pressure cuffs. After the vitals came the doctor's small parade. He shared my labs, told me whether my counts had inched up or dipped down, and set one new goal for the coming month. I liked having a target, something concrete to press toward. It helped my mind stay forward-looking rather than looping through worries.

Breakfast arrived on a covered tray. I prayed over the food, even on days when the smell turned my stomach. If I finished even half, that was a victory worth noting in my journal. Then it was time for a shower, a fresh T-shirt, and the morning reading. I opened my Bible and landed again and again on Psalm 91.

"He who dwells in the shelter of the Most High will rest in the shadow of the Almighty."

Those words sounded like a lullaby for grown folk. I read the psalm aloud, slow, letting each sentence settle, letting each promise answer the fear that still knocked on the door of my mind.

Chemo often dripped during that reading time. The pump beeped, and the medicine glided into the port beneath my skin. I pictured the chemo as a foot soldier, moving through my body hunting every last cancer cell. While the medicine worked, Scripture worked on my spirit, reminding me I was not fighting alone.

After the drip ended, I slept, sometimes for twenty minutes, other times for two hours, depending on how heavy the fatigue settled on my bones. Lunch came, followed by a slow stretch, and then the part of the day that made me feel alive: exercise.

***

The hallway in my unit formed a perfect oval loop. Twenty-five laps equaled a mile. I set that mile as my milestone early on. At first, I could barely finish ten laps without grasping the handrail. Slowly, I built endurance. On good days, I walked the full mile, headphones in, gospel playlist rolling. Travis Greene sang You Made a Way. Tasha Cobbs declared There is Power in the Name of Jesus. Each song pushed me one lap farther.

Back in my room, I faced the wall for push-ups, easing my arms into strength. Leg stretches next, then forty minutes on the exercise bike, the physical therapist had rolled in for me. Sweat poured, muscles burned, lungs fought for deeper breath, but when the timer chimed, I felt clearer, lighter, more in command of the body God was healing.

Exercise kept my mind from spiraling into loneliness. Yet loneliness did not disappear. When the room grew quiet and evening shadows lengthened, the ache of isolation pressed hard. I missed the ordinary chaos of home: my daughters arguing over the bathroom mirror, the smell of Barry's Saturday barbecue, the thump of old-school R&B drifting from the living room speaker. The silence of the ward, broken only by distant monitor alarms, sometimes felt endless.

On those nights, I reached again for Scripture. Psalm 91 settled me when anxiety climbed. I recited every verse, pairing the words with slow breaths. Inhale, "He will cover you with his feathers." Exhale, "Under his wings you will find refuge." Little by little, the knot in my chest untied itself, and I remembered I was never truly alone.

***

After months indoors, my doctor finally cleared me to work in the yard at home, masked and gloved, as long as the pollen count stayed low. That first afternoon outside felt like stepping into a gospel song. Sunlight warmed my scalp. I knelt beside the flowerbed and eased marigold seedlings into soft earth. Each plant felt like a prayer set in soil.

I had just rinsed the garden dirt from my hands and settled onto the porch swing, still smelling marigold on my fingertips, when the phone rang. It was a shaky voice from the office. My coworker was gone. Cancer again. Three weeks earlier, we had laughed about how we would order extra fries and split a slice of lemon cake once our treatments were behind us. Now the line crackled with finality. I pressed the phone to my chest, bent forward, and rocked until the boards beneath my feet creaked. Grief drifted in like a heavy fog, thick and cold. I could almost hear her voice telling me, *Keep going, girl. Live every minute wide open, just like we planned.* My throat tightened, but I whispered back, "I will, sis. I promise." Then I closed my eyes and prayed comfort over her husband and children, asking God to hold them the way He kept holding me.

Just as I was starting to breathe through that loss, the phone rang again two weeks later. Another death, this time inside the family circle. The blow fell harder, hitting a place so deep it felt physical. Fear leaned in close, whispering that my name might be next on some unseen list. I tried to pray, but every word came out like a sigh. For two full days, I moved through the house in a gray drift, watering plants, reheating soup, staring at walls, barely aware of my own steps. Even the flowers seemed to droop in sympathy.

On the third morning, I reached for my Bible with hands that trembled. I turned to First Thessalonians, the passage about hope that stretches beyond the grave. I read it aloud once, twice, a third time, letting the syllables settle into my bones. With each repetition, the words carved themselves deeper, like Scripture-stone inside my chest: We do not grieve like those who have no hope. I pictured my loved ones stepping into light, whole and pain-free, their laughter rising higher than any hospital ceiling. Angels got their wings. That truth did not erase my sorrow, but it anchored my feet. I closed the Bible, set it in my lap, and whispered, "Lord, give me strength to keep walking." Then I stood, wiped tears with the back of my hand, and stepped off the porch, determined to put one foot in front of the other and live the day they no longer could

***

Even in the thick of it, there were moments of unexpected encouragement. Sometimes, it was just a glance or a few words from another patient that reminded me I wasn't alone. We were all walking our own version of the same path, and even small moments of quiet strength from someone else helped lift my spirit when I needed it most.

Sometimes encouragement came from the nurses. The nursing staff had a way of comforting without needing to say much. Every now and then, I'd hear a gospel song playing softly in the hallway or someone humming a familiar tune, and it felt like a small reminder from God that He was still near.

Evenings were usually quiet, but not silent. I often watched a favorite TV show just to hear familiar voices or called one of my sisters to talk about nothing in particular. Sometimes I didn't have the strength to talk, so I just played soft music and let it fill the empty spaces. Vanessa Bell Armstrong, Yolanda Adams, and old Kirk Franklin kept me company when words failed me.

My days followed the same structure, and at first, that repetition wore me down. But over time, I realized how much I needed the rhythm. The predictability became my foundation. Knowing what came next gave me something solid to hold onto. That's how I learned to celebrate the little victories. Finishing breakfast. Making it through all twenty-five laps. Smiling at a nurse even when I didn't feel like it. Every small win became a reason to give thanks.

During support meetings held virtually with other patients, I found myself sharing more than I expected. One day, someone new joined the call. She looked scared, just like I had been when this started. I told her, "I've been where you are, and you are not alone. This fight is not easy, but it's not impossible." After the session, the facilitator messaged me privately and thanked me for encouraging the group. I didn't even realize my words mattered. But maybe that's the beauty of walking through fire, you can light someone else's way.

***

There's something strange about grieving while trying to heal. The weight of loss presses down even as you're fighting to hold yourself up. That season of back-to-back deaths shook my soul. I would walk to the window and stare out, wondering why God left me here. Why did I get to keep breathing while so many others didn't? That guilt was real. It was heavy. I had to learn not to carry it.

I often found myself talking to the people I lost in my prayers, in my thoughts. I'd whisper things I never got to say out loud. I'd thank them for loving me, for being part of my journey. I would ask God to give their families peace, and to help me carry their memory forward in strength.

I promised them I would keep going. I prayed over their families and asked God to give them the peace He was slowly giving me. Grief didn't leave, but it stopped screaming. It settled into something quieter, still painful, but more patient. And I kept moving, one day at a time.

1 Thessalonian 4:13-14 (NIV bible verse), *Believers who have died*

"Brothers and sisters, we do not want you to be uninformed about those who sleep in death, so that you do not grieve like the rest of mankind, who have no hope. For we believe that Jesus died and rose again, and so we believe that God will bring with Jesus those who have fallen asleep in him."

Chapter 5
Moving Forward

Isiah 43:18-19 Remember ye not former things, neither consider the things of old. Behold, I will do a new thing; now it shall spring forth; shall ye not know it? I will even make a way in the wilderness and rivers in the desert.

I had a clinical appointment in a few days, and I was already starting to feel off balance. At first, I thought I might have just overexerted myself during a workout, so I told myself I'd rest for a couple of days. But when I woke up this morning, my eyes were yellow, and I felt scared. At the clinic, I checked in and had blood work done, but I started to feel weak almost immediately. I wondered if maybe the cancer was coming back. The nurse came in and told me to go straight to the ER. They already had my admission order ready. It felt like a step backward, a moment that forced me to lean on God again for whatever was coming.

When I arrived at the emergency room, they took me straight in and helped me change into a hospital gown. A team of people came in to perform ultrasounds of my organs and an X-ray. I learned that I had gone into renal failure and that I had jaundice. I reached out to my family and friends to let them know I was back in the hospital again. I didn't tell my daughters because this was their first concert and their first real outing in two and a half years.

My daughters stayed in the house with me and didn't leave my side except for work and school. They were so excited to attend the concert with their cousin, and I was happy for them. I told them I had errands to run, and I wouldn't be able to make it home to see them off before they left. If I had told them, they would not have gone to the concert. So, I turned my phone off because I knew they had a tracker on my phone that would show my location at the hospital. When my daughters came back home, I asked my husband to explain what was going on. I asked him to be honest and to let them call me with any questions. I am human, and I feared what might lie ahead.

I thought about my daughters getting ready for that concert while I was lying flat on a hospital gurney waiting for test results. Even from the ER, I could picture them at home fussing over outfits, arguing about which lip gloss lasted longer, borrowing earrings from each other's jewelry trays. They hadn't had a single carefree night in two-and-a-half years. Anywhere I went, they went: clinics, pharmacies, late-night drugstore runs, bleary-eyed morning drives to early chemo. Tonight was supposed to be different.

Earlier, when they called to double-check whether they should stay home, I could hear the hesitation in Makayla's voice. "Mom, are you sure you don't need us?" she asked for the third time. I swallowed the sting of guilt and smiled into the phone. "Go have fun," I said. "Text me when you get there. Send pictures." My hands were already trembling from the IV line, but I kept my voice bright and steady. They deserved a night full of music, neon lights, and teenage freedom more than they could ever know.

From the ER bed, I watched the clock inch forward. A nurse was drawing blood, but my mind was miles away: imagining them in the car with their cousin, windows cracked, music turned up, finally laughing like girls their age again. That picture made my eyes water—half from joy, half from heartache so I angled my face toward the curtain so the nurse wouldn't see.

I kept replaying the moment I'd lied and said, "I've got errands." The lie felt small compared to everything we had survived, yet it sat on my chest like a brick. Still, a mother's job is equal parts truth and protection, and tonight protection had won. I whispered a quick prayer: "Lord, let them dance. Block every worry until morning."

About an hour later, my phone buzzed with the first blurry selfie: three happy faces under the arena marquee, cheeks pressed together, tickets in hand. I zoomed in on their eyes—the same eyes that had studied my pill bottles and lab reports for years—and saw nothing but excitement. I closed my own eyes and thanked God for that momentary gift.

Between ultrasounds, the phone kept lighting up with video clips: shaky concert lights, off-key singing, Makayla's laughter ringing louder than the bass. I pressed each clip to my heart like a secret talisman, letting their joy drown out the beeping monitors around me.

When pain stabbed through my side, I focused on my breathing, the way my meditation coach taught me: Inhale peace, exhale fear. With each exhale, I pictured sending a wave of protection over the girls, covering them in a bubble of carefree teenage bliss.

I did feel bad for hiding the truth, but I reminded myself I could shoulder a few hours of discomfort and sort the honesty out tomorrow. Tonight belonged to them. Tomorrow morning, after the music faded and their ears stopped ringing, we would sit in our living room with mugs of hot tea, and I would tell them everything: the jaundice, the renal scare, the next steps. We would cry, we would pray, and we would plan.

That thought steadied me. The IV pump clicked, the lab doors swung, but inside I found a quiet resolve. My girls were out there living, and I was right here in this hospital, fighting. Two battles, one family, same purpose: life.

My nephew Anthony came to visit to make sure I was okay and to see if I needed anything. Little does Anthony know, I just wanted family love and support. He made my day because it helped me focus on other things. It was joyful to see him and joke with him, regardless of my situation. My brothers, Henry and Joe, provided love and comfort, filling in as supportive father figures.

My visit with Deacon Chambers was comforting. Although he had a family engagement out of town, he turned around to see me. His son mentioned that I must be a caring person if he made that visit. I could only smile because I needed that support as I was feeling down. Deacon Garner followed up with calls and visited me. As always, the compassion, love, and support were reassuring.

I beat the odds once again as I was discharged from the hospital. I found that the motivation to face cancer can be incredibly challenging, yet it also presents an opportunity for growth and renewal. Here are some ideas to help me move forward: Focus on my strengths- reflect on the resilience and strength I've demonstrated during my battle with cancer. This strength is the foundation for my future endeavors. **Set new goals-** establish personal goals that excite me, whether they relate to health, career, or personal interests. Having something to strive for can reignite my passion for life. **Connect with others**—surround myself with supportive people. Sharing experiences and listening to others can provide encouragement and inspiration. **Practice mindfulness**—meditation can help me stay present and appreciate the small joys in life, making it easier to move forward. Celebrate small victories—acknowledge and celebrate achievements, no matter how minor. Each step forward is a victory worth recognizing. **Explore new interests**—discover new hobbies and passions. **Volunteer or give back**—helping others can provide a sense of purpose and fulfillment. Look for opportunities to volunteer in my community or support cancer-related initiatives.

Create a vision board to visualize my dreams and aspirations, just as I did with my children and my friend Tamika. Seek professional guidance by speaking with a life coach to help process my experiences and develop a plan for moving forward. **Embrace change** by understanding that life after cancer may appear different, and that's okay. Accept these changes and view them as opportunities for new beginnings. Remember, healing is a journey, and it's perfectly fine to take it one step at a time. My story is robust, and my next chapter is waiting to be written, so stay tuned for my next big thing.

My odds of beating cancer tell a powerful story of resilience, hope, and determination. I had to confront this battle while sharing inspiring accounts of survival and strength. Advances in medical research, innovative treatments, and supportive care have greatly improved outcomes for many cancer patients. Key factors contributing to overcoming cancer include early detection, personalized treatment plans, support systems, healthy lifestyle choices, research and clinical trials, advocacy, and awareness. Together, these elements create a pathway for many to defy the odds and reclaim their lives after a cancer diagnosis. This includes my personal stories of triumph and resources for support.

Chapter 6
More than a Survivor

James 2:17 Faith by itself, if it is not accompanied by action, is dead.

When I reflect on how far I've come, I know that merely surviving wasn't enough. Surviving was the beginning. God didn't bring me through the fire just for me to sit still. I needed to use what I'd endured to uplift others, to reach people who were feeling alone in their pain, and to become a voice for the voiceless. While cancer ravaged my body, it also sharpened my focus. It refined my purpose like gold in the furnace. I transformed from being just a patient. I became an advocate, a professional, and a vessel of purpose.

Cancer didn't erase who I was. It uncovered more of me.

Professionally, I've always been a hard worker. I didn't start at the top; I built my way up. I started in administrative roles, learning how to keep things running, how to support others, how to manage the little details that make the big picture possible. Then I advanced to fiscal management. I learned how to manage money, how to create accountability, how to train others to do the same with excellence. Eventually, I became a Senior Grant & Fiscal Manager at Virginia Commonwealth University's Institute for Drug and Alcohol Studies. I managed millions in grant funding, not just the dollars, but the dreams and deliverables behind them. I helped guide strategic operations and trained teams in financial compliance, pushing for accuracy, integrity, and performance.

When I moved on to work with the Virginia Department of Environmental Quality, I stepped into another level of leadership. As a Senior Financial Services Analyst, I was developing strategies to improve service delivery. I wasn't just crunching numbers; I was building systems that made people's lives better. I always believed that no matter what role I had, the work I did should serve people. And through every title, every email, every long night at the desk, I carried that belief with me.

But the moment that reshaped everything came when I stepped into entrepreneurship. In 2025, I launched Fowler-Simmons Associates, LLC. I didn't take that step lightly. It wasn't just about starting a business. It was about starting over on my own terms. I had spent years giving my talents and skills to organizations, and now I wanted to pour them into a vision that reflected my heart. As the founder and business owner, I oversee daily operations, negotiate contracts, and lead financial planning. But what drives me more than anything is the mission: to build a legacy grounded in service, excellence, and community uplift. My business isn't just about profit. It's about purpose. It's about reclaiming my time, my gifts, and my voice. It's about showing that even after a diagnosis tried to stop me, I'm still standing, and I'm still building.

This business was a milestone, but it was also something deeper. It was an act of healing. It reminded me that I am still powerful. I am still resourceful. I am still resilient. Cancer didn't take my brilliance. It didn't take my mind. It didn't take my work ethic. I poured all that I had learned over decades of leadership, budgeting, and community service into a venture that now serves others with integrity.

But beyond the workplace, my soul found its greatest reward in service.

Yet, my heart's true calling has always been in my volunteer service. Titles and paychecks matter, but what I do for God's people, that's where my real joy lives. I serve as a Deacon at St. Paul's Baptist Church, and that role carries weight, not just in name, but in responsibility. It's not just about sitting on the front row on Sundays. It's about counseling people through real-life storms, listening when someone has no one else, and walking beside those who feel like they've lost their way.

Whether it's ministering to someone who just got bad news or guiding a young person through a spiritual crisis, I show up with my whole heart. I've facilitated youth programs, encouraged prayer among the brokenhearted, and reminded people that no matter how far they feel from God, He hasn't gone anywhere. Sometimes, it's just about being a quiet presence, someone who says, "You are seen. You are loved. You are not alone."

My faith didn't shrink after my diagnosis; it grew stronger roots. Cancer may have threatened my body, but it could not steal my purpose. If anything, it sharpened it. That's why I dedicate so much of my time to organizations that fight for the same things I do: healing, equity, and awareness. I volunteer with the Leukemia & Lymphoma Society, using my own testimony to support other patients and their families. I've stood beside them, offered prayer, and shared what I've learned to help ease their fears.

I've also become a part of the American Cancer Society's Voices of Black Women initiative, a movement that speaks directly to the disparities our community faces in health care. When I speak to other Black women, it's not with statistics—it's with truth. With love. With understanding. I know what it's like to feel overlooked or unheard in a doctor's office. That's why I share my story—not for sympathy, but for change. Because change doesn't start in the headlines—it starts in the waiting rooms.

At VCU Massey Comprehensive Cancer Center, I serve as a Cancer Champion and clinical trial advocate. This role has allowed me to educate, inspire, and empower patients, especially those hesitant about trials because of past injustices. I help explain what trials are, why informed consent matters, and how these medical advances can open doors. I want people to know that knowledge is power, and when it comes to your health, you deserve the truth, the options, and the support to decide what's best for you.

It doesn't stop there. I support the work of the Association of American Cancer Institutes by helping raise awareness about initiatives like SIRUM, which works to redistribute unused medicine to those in need. I'm also proud to serve on the Community Advisory Board for the cancer pain and opioids education projects at Massey. Because when people are in pain, they need care, not silence. They need answers, not stigma.

In March 2025, I was proud to help submit an abstract for the APHA 2025 Annual Meeting & Expo, one of the largest and most respected gatherings in the public health world. Just being part of something like that was meaningful, but it wasn't just about showing up—it was about contributing to the conversation in a way that mattered.

Our abstract, titled "Measuring Community Engagement in Research: Insights from the Cancer Champs Program," reflected everything I stand for: representation, education, and involvement at the community level. This wasn't theory or speculation. This was about real people, real stories, and the impact of authentic connection in cancer care. We wanted to show that community engagement is not just a checkbox—it's the foundation for trust, especially in Black and brown communities that have been historically mistreated or ignored by the medical system.

When I think about how far I've come, from lying in a hospital bed wondering if I'd survive, to co-authoring an abstract submitted to a national health expo, I'm reminded that God can take what was meant to destroy you and use it to uplift others. That's what purpose looks like.

And it didn't stop there.

In May 2025, I participated in AACI/AACR Hill Day, where I sat across from members of Congress and told my story, not just as a patient, but as an advocate, a mother, a professional, and a believer in change. I talked to them about why NIH and NCI funding must be protected and expanded. I told them that cancer doesn't wait, and neither can we.

There I was, in a room where decisions are made, using my voice to speak not only for myself but for the thousands of others who might not have the platform, the access, or the strength in that moment to speak. That day reminded me that faith and action go hand in hand. Like the Scripture says, "Faith without works is dead." I couldn't just pray for better outcomes, I had to show up and be part of the change.

I also took part in Clinical Trials Day, where I shared my experience and helped demystify the clinical trial process for others who were unsure or afraid. I explained what I had learned, how I had prayed over every decision, and how I walked into each appointment with both faith and facts. I wanted people to understand that clinical trials are not about being experimented on, they're about finding answers, and in some cases, they're about giving someone else a fighting chance.

I've also supported efforts to lower prescription drug prices, especially for life-saving treatments that people simply cannot afford. Because access to care should not be based on your income. Life is sacred, and healing should never come with a price tag that robs people of their dignity.

Everything I've experienced, every needle, every diagnosis, every time I sat in a cold hospital gown waiting for a result, led me here. I didn't walk through this valley just to survive it. I came out on the other side because I was meant to do something with what I'd been through. To carry the lessons. To share the truth. To reach back and help someone else who may feel like giving up.

I speak from experience. Not statistics. Not theory. I speak as a woman who has stared death in the face and still decided to show up to serve.

The truth is, cancer took a lot from me. My energy. My independence. My hair. My time. But it didn't take my voice. It didn't take my faith. And it did not take my purpose.

These days, I find myself looking at life differently. I see beauty in the ordinary things, hearing my daughters laugh, making breakfast without feeling pain, walking to the mailbox with steady steps. These are victories. I don't wait for big milestones to feel grateful anymore. I celebrate the small wins, because they're the foundation of my strength.

And while the world may see me as a survivor, I know that title doesn't capture the fullness of who I am. I am more than a survivor.

I am a woman who walks with God. A mother who kept going. A leader who rose. A fighter who never let fear have the final word.

This journey has shown me what resilience truly looks like, not loud or flashy, but quiet, steady, and faithful. It's waking up each morning, choosing to live with intention, and saying, "God, use me today."

So if you're reading this and you're in your own storm, if your body is tired or your heart is heavy, know this: you are not alone. There is purpose in your pain. There is power in your persistence. And there is peace waiting for you on the other side of surrender.

Keep going. Keep showing up. Keep trusting God to do what only He can.

You are more than what you're facing.

You are more than a survivor.

The Now

Proverbs 22:2 Rich and poor have this in common: The Lord is the maker of them all.

It has always been a challenge for women of color to be truly heard regarding our health. We face many obstacles, from double standards in the healthcare system to racism, bias, and unfair judgment. My goal is to raise awareness about the importance of annual exams and screenings. The aim is for primary care doctors to run blood tests that can detect potential blood cancer abnormalities early. The fight isn't over; we need to get this house bill approved and passed. My motto is simple: Help one, save one life, so no one else must endure the storm of late stage cancer like I did. We must find ways to stay one step ahead of this disease and cross that line into victory. To fight this battle, I have joined the VCU Cancer Champion programs, One Team, One Fight, and become an American Cancer Society Voices of Black Women Ambassador, as well as volunteered with the Leukemia & Lymphoma Society.

My favorite quote from Shirley Chisholm still lights a fire in me: "If they don't give you a seat at the table, bring in a folding chair. We must reject not only the stereotypes that others hold of us, but also the stereotypes that we hold of ourselves." That quote reminds me that we don't have to wait for permission to take up space. We do not need to shrink ourselves just to make others feel comfortable. We are worthy of being seen, being heard, and being counted, fully and without compromise.

As I move forward in this chapter of my life, I think a lot about legacy. Not just the kind you leave in your bank account or on a resume, but the one you pass down in your values. What do my children take from watching me walk through this? I hope they remember my strength, but I also want them to remember the importance of truth. Integrity. Being able to look yourself in the mirror at night and know you stood by your values, even when no one else was watching. Because one day, if they become parents, their children will look to them as role models, just as mine look to me. And what they see will shape the kind of people they choose to become.

I want them to know that financial planning matters. That building something stable for your family is not just a task but an act of love. I want them to hold on to our traditions, those meals, those gatherings, those laughs that make the hard days easier. And I want them to give back. Always. Because what we survive is never just for us. It's meant to serve someone else. We are blessed to be a blessing.

And while I stand strong in my faith and hope, I also won't pretend that trusting others has come easily through all of this. If anything, it has become harder. I've learned that people don't always tell the whole truth. They speak in fragments. They move in silence, and sometimes not for good reasons. I pay attention to energy now. I watch how people move, not just what they say. My instincts have never failed me. And once my trust is broken, that's it. I remove myself. I don't make announcements. I don't argue. I don't make a scene. I simply step away and protect my peace.

That's the thing about going through the fire. It refines you. It teaches you that not every connection deserves access. Not every person can go where God is taking you next. And that's alright.

There were many days I sat alone with my Bible and just let the pages fall open. Some days, the pain in my body was loud. But the pain in my spirit? That was louder. It would hum under the surface; sometimes fear, sometimes doubt, sometimes just the heaviness of carrying so much for so long. And I wouldn't always have the words. That's when I would go back to my journal, back to my scriptures, back to the verses that held me when I couldn't hold myself.

Psalm 91.

That was my shelter.

"He who dwells in the secret place of the Most High shall abide under the shadow of the Almighty."

I would whisper that to myself when I needed to feel covered, when I needed to feel safe. That Psalm reminded me that no matter what I was walking through, I wasn't walking through it alone.

Psalm 23 was always nearby too.

"The Lord is my shepherd…"

There was a power in saying those words aloud. They settled my nerves. They reminded me of who I belonged to.

There were others I kept close like armor—Psalm 25:5, Psalm 103:2-3, Isaiah 53:5, Philippians 4:13, 1 John 5:4, Deuteronomy 20:4, Psalm 6:2, Jeremiah 17:14.

Each one was a reminder. That I was already being healed, already being strengthened, already being covered.

And it wasn't just for me. That's the part people sometimes forget. Yes, I was walking through this valley, but I wasn't only carrying my own story. I was carrying the names of people I've met along the way. The ones who didn't make it. The ones still fighting. The ones too afraid to speak. I carried them all. In my prayers. In my actions. In my purpose.

That's why I show up when I do those advocacy meetings. Why I go into rooms with people in suits and speak plain truth. I carry those who can't be there. I stand for those still lying in hospital beds, waiting for hope to knock.

Because I am more than a survivor.

I am a servant. A steward. A warrior with scars and purpose.

So if you are reading this, I want you to hear me clearly.

Don't wait until your body is broken to pay attention.

Don't wait until the doctor says, "We caught it too late."

Get your checkups. Speak up when something doesn't feel right.

And when fear creeps in, because it will, remember who you are and whose you are.

I made it through because I held onto my faith, even with trembling hands.

I walked through fire and came out stronger, wiser, and ready to tell it.

Not just that I survived. But that I lived. Fully, intentionally, with grace and with grit.

This is my now.

And I'm not done yet.

The Disparity

Please note that African Americans in the United States face significant disparities across various aspects of society, often rooted in historical and ongoing systemic racism and discrimination. Although I recognize we are not the only race experiencing injustices, I can only speak on my own race and the hardships my ancestors endured.

African Americans experience worse health outcomes than White people, including higher rates of chronic diseases like heart disease, stroke, cancer, asthma, and diabetes. Unfortunately, we often do not receive respectful treatment in healthcare, and issues with trust and communication persist. We frequently encounter physicians who don't listen to us, as if we are not knowledgeable about our bodies or how we feel, especially regarding reactions to medication. The trust problem is serious because racism continues; I thought times had changed, but division remains. You are told one thing, yet falsehoods can lead to different actions. As a community, we need to identify who can be trusted to move forward. Race influences medical education and clinical decisions through provider biases and race-based factors in tools and algorithms. African Americans face significant financial barriers to healthcare access and report experiencing discrimination and disrespect from healthcare providers. These are substantial obstacles to receiving quality care and overcoming biases in medical settings. Frankly, some elders and others in our community did not feel safe visiting the doctor until President Barack Obama took office. Our First Lady, Michelle Obama, prioritized healthy eating, exercise, affordable healthcare, and regular doctor visits. President Obama's time in office brought hope, vitality, and joy for equality for all.

African Americans have a noticeably lower life expectancy than white people. This is because we are often ignored, and trust in healthcare is broken. African American women are more likely to die from pregnancy-related causes, and Black infants have higher mortality rates than white infants. Doctors often overlook blood tests or fail to understand the patient's medical history during treatment. For example, I had preeclampsia and low iron levels, but they were ignored. I managed to get through it by the grace of God. The terms are maternal and infant mortality.

Impact of Disparities:

These disparities have major effects, influencing the physical and mental health, economic stability, educational success, and overall well-being of African Americans. Tackling these issues requires a comprehensive approach, including policy changes, increased investment in underserved communities, and efforts to combat systemic racism and implicit bias.

By recognizing the deep roots of these disparities and implementing targeted policies and innovations, society can work toward a more just and equitable future for all, making America a united and prosperous nation.

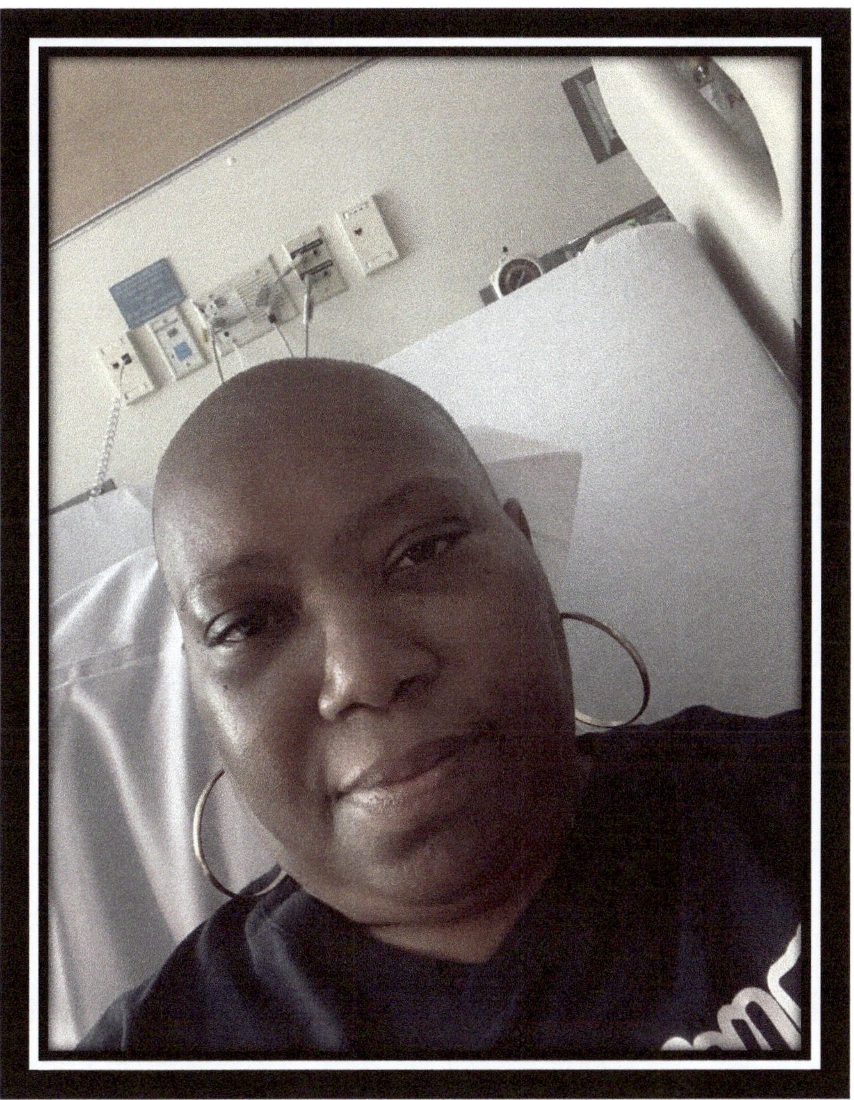

Acute Care Oncology at
VCU
Massey Cancer Center
Oncologica de Cuidado Agudo
en VCU Massey Cancer Center
Conector to
Main

84

Diane and I

Dr. Robert Winn (the influential leader at VCU Massey Comprehensive Cancer Center) and I

Dr. Keri Maher (my outstanding doctor) and I

Nicole Hansen and Family

My big brother and I (twins)

The brothers (Fowler Legacy)

My oldest and strongest sister is Josephine.

Please note that I recognize all my sisters (the warriors) and my brothers (legacy) because I haven't posted my whole family, as the love is within us

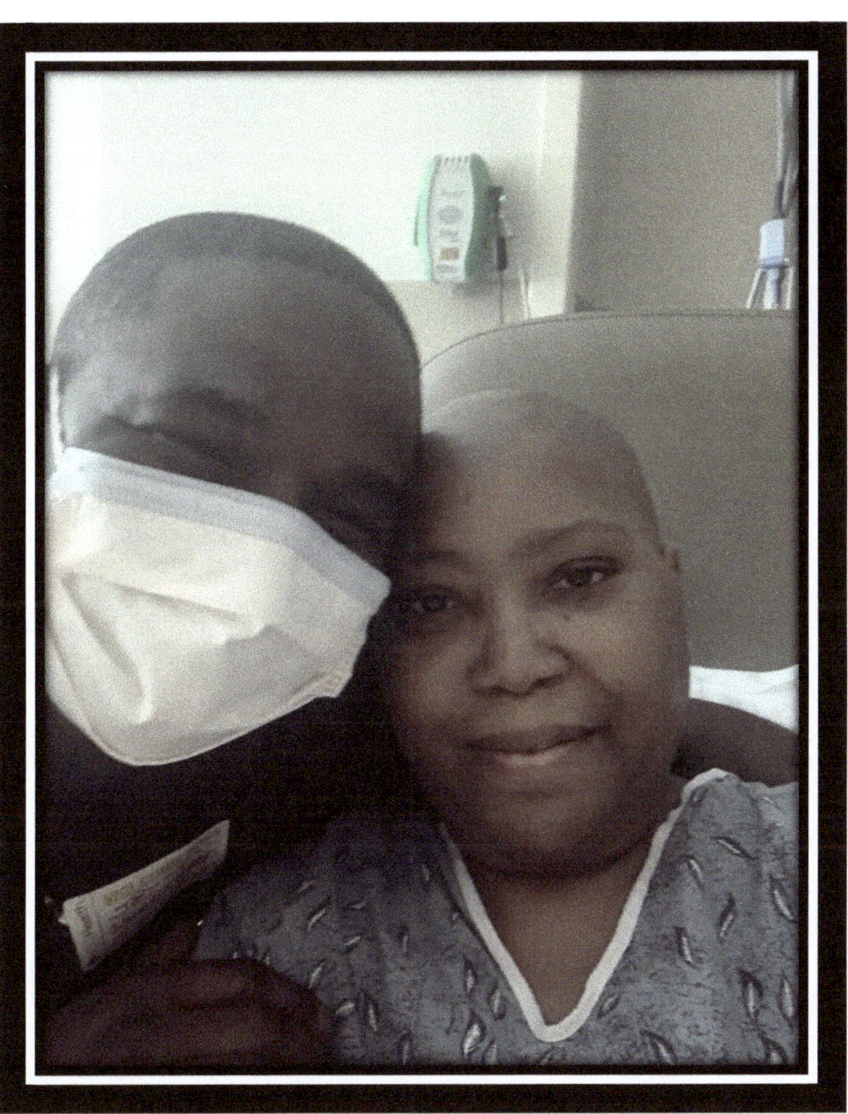

Reflections from my family

Barry's reflection (soulmates)

I faced a mix of emotions—shock, fear, and sadness—as I grappled with the reality of my wife's diagnosis. Concerns about her health, the impact on our family, and the uncertainty of the future weighed heavily on my mind. Over time, I had to accept the situation and take on a supportive role. I needed to focus on being there for my wife, both emotionally and physically. I couldn't guide my children because I felt shut down. My acceptance deepened my appreciation for our time together and fostered resilience in our relationship. I maintained a blend of hope and determination, wanting to fight alongside her through treatments and challenges.

Ultimately, acceptance can bring a sense of purpose, helping me appreciate the moments we share and find strength in our bond as we navigate this journey together. It was also crucial for me to seek support because of the heavy burden I was carrying alone.

Makayla's reflection (The Business Lady)

As the eldest of the three siblings, I always had to be independent and strong-willed. I was able to step in for my mom and try to fill her shoes while she was in the hospital. I received help from my mom's support network, but it became challenging. I'm a college student, and I had to juggle a household that involved looking after my younger siblings, cooking, cleaning, buying groceries, paying bills, and trying to support my father as he was falling apart. My shoulders felt heavy, and I had no safe corner to let it all out. My mind searched for a resolution, but it became more difficult each day. I spent my alone time in the shower to release my feelings or in bed, lying in the dark and crying quietly. It was even harder to watch my mom suffer in her fragile state. I had to be strong and look past the illness. I needed to be brave for her and for myself, even though I was hurting inside. I became her caretaker, helping with her clinical appointments, being at her bedside for every procedure, picking up her medications, and maintaining my grades as a college student. Everything became a routine; I grew numb and did what needed to be done. My mom's health was very uncertain, and it was painful to watch her go through various medical procedures. Each day, I woke up thinking I was living in a nightmare. I can't imagine any loss as I continued to pray for our family. I felt tempted to drop out of college to work and take care of my mom. I knew she would be upset if she knew how I felt. My mom always told me to cry it out and move forward. Life is never forgotten, but we must continue to live it to the fullest.

Kiyah's reflection (The Social Worker)

I am the middle child of three siblings. I felt pain, rage, frustration, and loss. I woke up feeling numb as I continued to be isolated. I'm a senior in high school, and not being able to share my day with my mom hurt me. I didn't know how to act or what to do. My big sister tells me to come out of the room for dinner and movie night on the weekend. I knew this was what Mom would want us to do. I hated seeing my mom sick and just wanted to do anything I could to help her get better. I graduated from high school, and my mom was still in the hospital. My Aunt Diane and my cousin Tierra stood in for my mom. Bernita, my mom's friend, sent me edible arrangements on my graduation day. My mom cheered me on as she watched virtually and called me as soon as I got home. I want my mom back healthy so that we can do family activities together again.

Mya's reflection (The Artist)

I am the youngest of three siblings. My mom pampered me with love but was also strict. Hearing my mom's terminal diagnosis broke my heart and left me at a loss for words. On weekends, we always had family outings or exciting activities. My mom made things happen; she consistently created fun experiences for us. She organized a family paint day in our backyard, grilling food and listening to soulful music. Naturally, I won the art show because I am the artist in the family. We went on trips to museums, parks, college basketball games, and out to dinner. This journey we were on felt like a roller coaster that no one should want to experience because that's how my emotions felt.

Tierra Fowler (Big Baby)

"No one ever wants to see the people they love hurt. Looking back at seeing the person who helped raise and knows you inside out, having received a cancer diagnosis was a pain I could never fully explain. My only goal at the time was to get to my aunt as quickly as possible. Seeing her in a hospital bed made me feel so helpless, and there was nothing I could do. In hindsight, the hardest part was keeping it together while there. This situation has taught me how big our God is. With prayer and her own will to push through, she gave me strength. I learned that even a woman small in stature had the determination of a thousand strong men. She was able to undergo treatment and work out, all while maintaining a positive attitude. I've never seen her flinch or show any weakness. She knew she had to be there for her girls and continue to speak life into herself. I realized how mighty she was, is, and the God she served.

Marcus (nephew and the peacemaker)

Coco

George and Pat

As a caring sister in Christ, I provided practical and emotional support to Mary and her family. I understood the importance of being present, listening actively, helping with meals, transportation, errands, and offering ongoing support. I remember her as the person she was, not just a cancer patient; maintaining our love in our relationship was essential. It was okay to acknowledge that cancer is difficult and to offer my shoulder to cry on, but I also stayed in prayer for her. I offered encouragement and shared positive experiences from her life while avoiding making life comparisons. I stayed in touch through calls, texts, or visits, even when she wasn't feeling well. I was not afraid of silence because being present and allowing quiet moments are helpful. Respecting her privacy and understanding boundaries allowed her the space for rest or to be alone. George and I remain supportive and offer encouragement to our extended family.

The Diva Deacons

Acknowledgments

I want to thank God first for guiding me through this journey. To my family, friends, and prayer warriors; your love carried me through every high and low. I also want to thank the team at Fawcett for helping me complete this book. I was truly blessed with a team that understood my vision, respected my voice, and handled this story with care and compassion. This story is a piece of my heart, and I'm grateful to everyone who stood beside me while I wrote it.